MY FAIR LADY

Monica Dickens

Adapted from the musical play by
Alan Jay Lerner and Frederick Loewe

SBS SCHOLASTIC BOOK SERVICES
New York Toronto London Auckland Sydney

This edition published by Scholastic Book Services, a division of Scholastic Magazines, Inc., by arrangement with CBS Films, Inc.

A hardcover edition of this book is published by Four Winds Press, a division of Scholastic, and is available through your local bookstore or directly from Four Winds Press, 50 West 44 Street, New York, New York 10036.

1st printing   September 1968

Printed in the U.S.A.

Chapter 1

SHE WAS CHRISTENED Elizabeth Doolittle, but nobody ever called her that.

Her mother called her Bessie, because she had named her after Queen Elizabeth of England — "Good Queen Bess" — who was one of the few characters in history she knew.

Her father, Alfred Doolittle, a large man with a red face and a loud beery voice, called her Eliza, after the girl in one of his favorite songs: *"Eliza, Eliza, the presents I buys 'er, she throws 'em right back in me face."*

The other children who played with her in the filthy slum streets that ran in and out like shabby mongrel terriers under the legs of the black railway arches called her Lizzie.

The Doolittle family lived in a gray brick

terrace house in Lisson Grove, in a part of London which was never much before the trains, and lost hope completely after the line was cut through. Their two rooms on the top floor back were on a level with the railway viaduct, so that the trains ran right outside the windows and showered Eliza's geraniums with sticky black soot. When the wind was not blowing the smoke that way, she could look into the lighted carriage windows and see the ladies, mysterious in their traveling veils, and the gentlemen with their side whiskers growing down into their high collars, too deep in the newspaper to notice Eliza's pale face behind the dirty glass and the dying geraniums. But she would imagine herself in there with them, rattling away to the north, and think, "One day, I'll go somewhere too."

The year was 1900. A bad year for jobs, Alfred Doolittle said, although every year seemed to have been that, as long as Eliza could remember. He was a lazy, boastful man, whose tongue was the only part of him that got enough exercise. Always in and out of work, and mostly out, if there was any money to spare in the cracked case on the mantelpiece, he would take it off to the Red Lion public house and get rid of it in beer or bets on horses.

Eliza's mother took in sewing to keep them all alive. She often worked late into the night, peering under the dim lamp, until the gray morning crept in, and the mail trains came whistling down into London. Out of the left-over pieces of ladies' gowns, she made pretty dresses for her Bessie to wear at school, "So she can look like the queen she is." She was very proud of her daughter, who was quick and clever. Eliza learned to read and write at the shabby little school, though not much else, because in those days not much else was taught to children of the poor, especially if they were girls.

"She'll grow up to be something better than us one day, you'll see," Eliza's mother told her husband, but Alfred Doolittle only said, "I don't see there's anything wrong with *me*."

It was in the bitterly cold winter when Eliza was fourteen that her mother grew ill and could not leave her bed. Her father was off somewhere chasing one of the "golden opportunities" that he always knew were waiting for him round the next corner. Eliza was afraid to get the doctor because there was no money to pay him. She spent the last pennies in the vase to buy bones to make soup which her mother could not swallow, and crept up to the railway yards at night to steal enough coal to keep the fire going, because her mother was so cold all the time, except when she was burning hot.

One evening she did not get warm, and she did not move or speak, and Eliza knew that she was dead. When her father came home, Eliza told him, "You killed her!" and he went into a noisy show of grief, waking the neighbors. But it was Eliza who went out and sold their table, so that her mother could have a proper funeral.

Now she was nobody's queen. Her father took her away from school and put her to work in a shirt factory, where she crouched in a basement room for ten hours a day, sewing thousands of buttons onto hundreds of shirts. There were other girls to talk and joke with, and songs to sing in the piercing cockney accents of the slum streets they came from.

My old man said, "Foller the van,
And don't dillydally on the wye."
Off went the van wiv me 'ome packed in it.
I followed on wiv me ol' cock linnet.
But I dillied and dallied,
Dallied and dillied. . . .

The other girls hated the shirt factory as much as Eliza did, but they stayed on there, because jobs were hard to find if you were a woman and didn't know anything. But Eliza had more spirit. Knocked down so often by life, she was like one of those weighted dolls that roll back upright every time. She had never lost that feeling that there must be something better than this for her. The feeling that had made her believe, when she saw the veiled ladies and whiskered gentle-men go rattling by in the trains, "One day I'll go somewhere too." She never forgot her mother saying, with her sweet tired smile, "Something better for her one day."

After a year, she ran away from the factory one spring morning when she could see the sun shining through the narrow windows which were on a level with people's boots and shoes as they walked by on the pave-ment. The manager ran after her, chasing her flying skirts through the crowds on the street, crying, "Stop, thief!" Her father had hired her to the factory for five years, so she was stealing his time.

"Stop, thief!"

The people did not think he meant Eliza, who looked too skinny and bedraggled to be a villain, so she escaped through the crowd into the park, where she spent two nights under the bushes and two days sharing thrown crusts with the sparrows and ducks, before she dared go home to her father.

After his wife's death, Alfred Doolittle had left the wretched rooms by the railway, and was lodging now in Euston Road — not grand, but better than Lisson Grove, because he had Eliza's meager wages to help with the rent.

He also had a steady job for the first time in his life. He called himself a "servant of the public," which could have meant any-thing from a politician to a rat catcher, but actually meant he was a dustman, emptying bins full of ashes and unspeakable things people threw out into his square yellow dust-cart which was drawn by a square white horse called Nora.

It was not like him to be in such regular work: Monday those streets, Tuesday these, Wednesday dump the whole lot in the River Thames, Thursday those other streets, Friday plod Nora to the office for his pay. But he rather fancied his landlady, and wanted to impress her.

Mrs. Prunella Hardcastle lived on the ground floor of her house in Euston Road, in which Alfred Doolittle, Public Servant, had a comfortable second-floor room, and his daughter Eliza a tiny attic, just wide enough to hold a rusty iron bed. When Eliza came nervously home, her father was having a cup of tea with Mrs. Hardcastle in the landlady's cosy kitchen, haunted by old smells of stews and kippers and Brussels sprouts, the ghosts of all the meals she had cooked for the late Mr. Hardcastle before his winter cough carried him off in 1897, the year of Queen Victoria's Diamond Jubilee.

Mrs. Hardcastle was an energetic, upright woman, like a soldier, with thick black hair puffed out high like a bearskin, and a mole in the dead center of her chin, sprouting one whisker at attention. The high collar of her blouse was held up on her neck with whalebones, and fastened with a huge shell brooch in which she could hear the sea. Mr. Doolittle had found it in someone's rubbish bin and brought it home to her with pride.

He was wearing his dustman's hat, close-fitting on the brow with a black flap behind to take the rub of the bins, a shirt without collar or tie, leather waistcoat flapping over Mrs. Hardcastle's digesting steak and chips, a piece of string round his trousers below the knee, and a pair of brown elastic-sided boots thrown out by Lord Roderic Jamieson at No. 101 Tavistock Square.

"So there she is." Mrs. Hardcastle looked at Eliza without pleasure. "Two nights gone, we thought we'd seen the last of you."

"Worried about me, Dad?" In the hideous event that Mrs. Hardcastle ever became her stepmother, Eliza might have to talk to her. Meanwhile, she'd save her breath.

"Off and on, old girl." Her father leaned back, thumbs in belt, fingers tapping his stretched stomach. "Payday, ain't it?" One hand reached out across the kitchen table, palm up, middle finger beckoning.

"Not for me. I chucked it."

"You what?" The floor of Mrs. Hardcastle's kitchen, never so secure since they ran the new Twopenny Tube underneath it, trembled as he crashed down the front legs of his chair.

"Got fed up." Eliza pretended to be casual, although the kitchen smells made her faint with hunger. "What's for tea then?"

"Nothing for them as ain't in work." Mrs. Hardcastle shut her lips in a grim bar.

"You can't send me back there," Eliza said, watching her father. " 'E'll put me in jug. What would that do to your reputation?"

"We never had you in jail, that's true." Mr. Doolittle was surprised to realize it.

"Always a first time," Mrs. Hardcastle said. "Take your eyes off them buns, young lady."

"Knock it off, Prunella." Mr. Doolittle was a generous man, if it involved no personal effort. "The kid's got to eat."

Mrs. Hardcastle shoved a plate of cold potatoes and gristly meat at Eliza, and while she ate like a starving dog, they discussed her as if she were not there.

"Ought to take the buckle end of me belt to 'er."

"Strapping don't do no good with that kind. Born bad, I always said."

"What's to be done with 'er? She's no good for nothing, except eat."

"Sweep the crossings . . . bootblack . . ."

"Kitchen maid . . ."

"Who'd have Eliza in their kitchen? She's always on about flowers. Send her up to Covent Garden Market, Alfred Doolittle. She can buy flowers there cheap and sell 'em off in the streets at profit."

"Whose profit, Mrs. Hard Bargain?" Eliza's father winked, and Mrs. Hardcastle chuckled like water gurgling down the sink and said,

"Get away with you!" as if he had paid her a compliment.

So Eliza Doolittle became a flower girl, and for three years she sold violets and roses and lilies of the valley and carnations for buttonholes and posies for lovers in the streets round the bustling central market, where fruit and flowers and vegetables were brought into the great city from all over the countryside. The theaters were nearby, and the Opera House, a palace of gold and red velvet. Eliza's flowers were often bought by elegant gentlemen in top hats and tails for glorious ladies in furs and jewels, with skin like cream and hair like silk, who never knew she existed, except as a grubby paw held out for their coins.

Her friends and companions were the other shrill, ragged women who sold flowers and matches and clothespins on street corners, and the rough brawny costermongers and market porters in caps and greasy knotted scarves, who carried towering piles of baskets on their heads, and could sling a hundredweight of potatoes in the air as easily as if it were a baby.

One of them was Billy — he had forgotten his second name, if he ever knew it. He was more muscle than brain, a simple giant with mild blue eyes and a thatch of yellow hair that Eliza cropped raggedly with the flower scissors she used on her own straggly brown locks. His heart was big, and he loved Eliza Doolittle as if she had been one of the silk and cream ladies whose wheels splashed them with mud as they sat on orange crates and watched the nobs drive by to the opera.

He got flowers for her cheap, or "free," which meant when the wholesaler wasn't looking. Once he brought her a bird in a little cage that he had "borrowed" from a drunken sailor asleep on a sack of pickling onions.

It was a lovebird, brilliant blue and green, named Joey. She kept him in her room, Mrs. Hardcastle or no Mrs. Hardcastle, and he greeted her with a chirrup when she came home late at night after offering her flower basket among the crowds coming out of the theaters. She would hang her shawl and her torn old jacket on the nail at the back of the door, and clamber along the bed, which was the only way to get to the window, where Joey's cage hung over the struggling plants on the sill. With the bird chattering on her shoulder and her elbows on the iron bed head, she would gaze out over the slate roofs and chimneys and washing lines, and wonder where it had all gone to, the dreams of freedom, the journeys, the "something better."

"We could marry old Billy," she told the bird, "and get away from 'im and 'er." She stuck out her tongue toward the kitchen where

Mrs. Hardcastle and her father were having a little late beer and a song.

"Billy boy, billy boy, billy boy, billy boy," said the bird, as she had taught him.

"But 'e's not much in the top story. What's to become of us, Joey?"

"Joey, Joey, Joey." His conversation was not brilliant.

"What's it all about?" And though she was hungry and dirty and unremarked among the city's millions, the moon silvered the chimney pots for her, and the stars were as much hers as anyone else's, and she could not help the feeling that somewhere . . . some day . . .

Chapter 2

"LEND US half a crown, Eliza."

"What do'you mean, lend? You've never paid me back the last half crown I lent you, or the one before that, or —"

"Ssh!" Eliza and her father were in the cabbage-scented hall of the house in Euston Road, and he jerked his head toward the kitchen door, behind which Mrs. Hardcastle waited, like a whaleboned spider, for her rent.

"She'll put us out on the street," he said in the nearest his voice could get to a whisper.

"Not me. I can pay me way."

"Come on, girl, be a good sport. I wouldn't ask you, only I had a bit of bad luck with that three-legged brute that called itself a horse.

Won't you help your pore old Dad? After all I've done for you. Fed you, clothed you, rocked you to sleep . . ." He honestly believed it, so it was not worth denying. "Taught you the elements of 'oomanity. The Lord put us in this world to help each other, I told you, so you should be glad to fulfill your what's-its-name by helping me."

Eliza sighed. "I've got a two-bob bit and three pennies. That's all I took today."

"Give us it, love. I'll give it back tomorrow — double. Sure as me name's A. Doolittle."

"If you're going to put it on a horse —" Eliza's hand stopped on its way into the pocket of her old jacket that had once been the top part of a man's dark suit, but now had a greenish shine to it, like mould on jam.

"Cross me heart."

She gave him the two-shilling piece and the three pennies, and grabbed him as he made for the front door. " 'Ere 'ere! Not to the boozer." She pushed him the other way, through the kitchen door.

"Hullo, Mr. D — this is a pleasant surprise!" Which it was to Mrs. Hardcastle, when she saw the money in his hand.

Eliza had just come in after being out on the streets all day in the first nippy winds of winter, but she would have to go out again, or there would be nothing for her supper. She heard her father and the landlady laughing, and the enviable chink of teacups. Half

the time Mrs. Hardcastle did not save anything for her.

In the dusky streets, the lamplighter went
before her, touching each globe with yellow
gaslight, as she wandered down to Covent
Garden again to see if Billy could find her
some flowers.

When she saw him, his pale face in the
flare of a naphtha torch on one of the stalls,
she stopped a few yards away behind a bar-
rowload of rotting cabbages. What had he
done wrong? Had someone found out about
those white carnations? He was talking to a
man in a soft country hat and a long tweed
coat with a kind of cape on the shoulders like
a roof to let off the rain. He could only be a
plain-clothes policeman, or what would he
want with old Bill?

She slipped through a pool of deep shadow
beyond the naphtha flare, and ducked behind
a pillar to hear what they were saying.

" 'E gimme a narf cra-own fer a narf duzzy
nornchis."

"Say it again, there's a good chap." The
man in the tweed coat was a toff, no mistake.
No copper talked posh like that. But they
were up to all sorts of tricks, the coppers, you
couldn't be too careful. Don't tell 'im, Bill,
she urged silently.

" 'E gimme a narf cra-own fer a narf duzzy
nornchis," Billy repeated obediently, a fool-
ish grin splitting his broad face like a great
sliced turnip.

"Yes . . . yes . . ." The gent had a note-book and pencil and was marking it down. "Mile End Road?" Billy looked blank. "Born there, I mean?"

" 'Sright."

"Go on talking."

That was enough to strike poor Billy as dumb as a bed leg. "Ow — I — er —" He gasped and swallowed. Eliza could see his Adam's apple rushing desperately up and down his brawny neck, as the strange man waited patiently, pencil poised.

"Are you having some sort of seizure, my good fellow?" The inquiry was civil enough, but you had the feeling that if it were a fit he would stand and watch, rather than call for help.

"Ask my girl," Billy stammered out. "She does the talkin'." He put out a hand as large as half a ham and pulled Eliza out from be-hind the pillar.

" 'Ow did you know I was there?" She jerked her arm away and stood angrily, legs apart and basket on hip, the cracked black sailor hat she wore winter and summer nod-ding over her eyes.

"I seen yer." Sometimes it seemed that Billy had an odd extra sense, to make up for not having much of the ordinary kind.

"You in trouble?" she asked him. "What's 'e got yer for?"

"Calm yourself," said the stranger. "We're just having a chat."

"That's what the copper said when 'e come after me cousin. Next thing we knew 'e was inside wiv two months 'ard."

" 'Ard?" The man was not rude, but he was not polite either. Just point-blank inquisitive.

" 'Ard labor, as well you know, Mr. Nosy Parker. And if you've come trying to get pore Bill to say something incrum — incorm —"

"Incriminating?"

"Don't take me up!" she flashed at him. "I'm as good as you. Comin' 'ere, attackin' a pore innocent boy as don't even know 'is own name . . . you're all the same, you beggars . . . ." She raved on, giving him the saw-toothed edge of her tongue, which years of shrieking and quarreling on the London streets had sharpened to the shrillest cockney.

"Fascinating . . . fascinating." His pencil stabbed and flicked at the paper, making signs that did not look like letters to her, if they had taught her right at school. And then he looked up with one eyebrow raised, tapping the pencil on the good white teeth that were all his own. "Er — Edgeware Road?"

She nodded, in spite of herself.

"Lisson Grove?" His lean head swooped down at her. In the gassy light of the flare, she noticed that he had very bright brown eyes, witty and questioning, before she drew back afraid, for what did he want with her? What did he know about her?

"Nah," she lied. "You got the wrong party. My people was all Islington folks."

"Funny." He shut his notebook. "I could have sworn to Lisson Grove." As he began to amble away, he turned to say over his tweedy shoulder, "with perhaps the lightest touch of Euston Road on top?"

Eliza spat at him like a cat, and Billy was shocked. His attitude had irritated her before. He was awed by the gentry. Too meek, too willing to play underdog so that they could call him "My man," and chuck him a three-penny bit for fetching them a cab.

"Don't you think 'e was a copper?"

Billy shook his head. Events had moved too fast for him, and he would speak no more.

"Well, 'e knows too much," Eliza said darkly. " 'E's bad luck. I wouldn't give 'im the time of day, meself. I wouldn't give 'im the dirt from under me fingerniles."

The next day, Eliza felt vaguely unhappy. It had turned colder, and she began to think of the long winter ahead, when the rain was chillier than the snow, and there was no escape from the wind which searched you out round corners and behind walls like your own bad conscience.

After she had forced herself groaning and muttering out of bed, and pushed through the bars of Joey's cage the lettuce leaves she had brought home for him last night, she jammed on her flat straw hat and walked a different way to the market, to try to break up the deadly sameness of another deadly day.

It was one of those thick London mornings when you can't see who you are much before noon, and the light from a busy little shop fell pleasantly on the street corner ahead. It was a flower shop. Two women, one quite young, one older, were arranging plants and jars of flowers in the window and on the shelves, chatting to each other, like old friends.

Although she spent all her days with flowers, and wouldn't give you tuppence for them on days when no one would buy, Eliza could not help stopping to look at the bright display of yellow and ginger-brown chrysanthemums in the shop window. On a card in one corner she could read: "GIRL WANTED." Who said school was a waste of time?

Boldly she went in at the door, which made a bell say "Ping!" and boldly she said to the backs of the two women, "I'm the girl you want."

They swung round. The eyebrows of the younger one went up. The eyebrows of the older one came down in a scowl.

"Get out of here!" She moved her arms as if she had a broom, sweeping Eliza away. "Get out of here, you street urchin, before I call the police!"

As Eliza ran off down the street, sobbing with rage, the fog tearing at her throat, the

"Ping!" of the bell on the closing door said, "*That* to you!"

Down in the market, the porters and some of the flower girls (all called girls, though most of them were fat old women who sat all day in Piccadilly Circus crying hoarsely, "Sweet vi-o-lets!" and "Luverly daffs!") were heating a billy-can of tea over a brazier full of glowing coke, to keep out the raw cold. Eliza joined them, hunching miserably by the fire, and when Billy passed her his mug, she did not even smile at him. She brooded there for some time, warming her hands round the chipped enamel mug, before she became aware that last night's stranger was in there too, in the circle round the fire, his hat tipped over his bright brown eyes, and a foggy drop on the end of his upper-class nose.

"Go on, Guv'nor," Charlie Price was saying. " 'Ow about me?"

"A-ow aba-out may?" The man imitated it carefully, like a child repeating a lesson. "Unmistakably Hoxton, I'd say."

" 'Struth, you can't fault 'im. Bet yer a screw of tobaccer yer can't guess —" old Arthur quavered, but the stranger interrupted with a brisk, "Selsey. You can't hide that Sussex burr," and Arthur blinked. "It's a ruddy miracle."

"Do me." "Guess me." "Where was I borned then?" The thickset men and the bundled up gap-toothed women clamored at him from all round the group, and more of the blokes and girls wandered over from other parts of the market to see what was up.

"I'm not a music-hall turn," the man said quite irritably. He had that way of being friendly one minute, and biting your head off the next, like a fickle dog or a spoiled child.

"What's the game then?" Charlie Price asked suspiciously. "If you can't make a living at it on the music 'alls, what's the sense of it?"

"I do make a living, my dear fellow, but not on the stage. I write books about language. I teach it at the University of London. I give private lessons in speech. I read papers before select groups of the intelligentsia. You do behold, in short" — he bowed slightly from his seat on an upturned cauliflower basket — "the world-famous Henry Higgins, Professor of Phonetics."

"What's that when it's at home?" Old Mabel asked rudely, leering at him out of her one good eye.

"The science of speech. The way people talk. I've studied it for years. You can probably tell if a man's Irish, or broad North Country. I can tell you what town he's from. If he's a Londoner, which is my specialty at the moment, I can tell you what district, sometimes even what street."

A bit out of their depth, the crowd shifted

and muttered uneasily, looking at each other to see what to say, and the stranger's noticing eye fell on Eliza, frowning over her mug of tea at the back of the group.

"We've heard nothing from Miss Lisson Grove today. You were vocal enough last night. Where's your tongue this fair morning?"

She stuck it out at him, and hoped it looked as bilious as it felt.

"Aha — the morning after. Well, it happens to the best of us."

"Speak for yourself," Eliza growled. "I never touched a drop in me life."

"What's up then?" Henry — what was his name? — Higgins smiled at her quite kindly. For all his outlandish talk, there were fleeting moments when you felt he might be almost human.

"I been slighted, that's what." She told him about the women in the flower shop, half unwilling to admit the hurt of it, half glad of his interest and the sympathy of the rest of them.

"Tchk, tchk." He clicked the perfect teeth. "But it's no surprise."

Eliza jumped up and faced him, bristling all over. She could even feel her hat brim quivering with rage. "You watch your tongue, mister! I may be no oil painting, but I don't look as bad as all that!"

"You may have seen yourself in shop windows," he said, guessing correctly that she had no mirror. "But have you ever listened to yourself?"

" 'Ow could I, yer stoopid —"

"If you came home with me, I could reproduce your dulcet tones on my recording machine. The marvels of phonographic science." (Half of what he said Eliza could not properly understand.) "But since I'll be dashed if I'll invite you home," he wrinkled his nose, "you'll have to take my word for it. It's not only the way you look, it's the way you talk."

"What's wrong with the way I say things?"

"Out of your own mouth! *'Wot's wrong wiv ve wye I sye fings?'* "

Although they all talked the same kind of broad cockney, the crowd round the fire bucket laughed, because it sounded so funny, coming out of the mouth of this surprising Higgins gent.

"What did I ought to 'ave said to them women?" Eliza backed away, as if they were laughing at her. She talked to the professor, and kept her eyes on him.

"Try this another time: 'Were you wanting extra help?' That would sound so nice and refined, they might not notice you weren't quite dressed for the part."

Eliza took a deep breath. "Were you —" That sounded wrong to her. "Was you wantin' hextra 'elp?"

"Was that what I said?"

"I'm not deaf, mister. Was you wantin' hextra 'elp?"

He screwed up his face as if he'd bitten on a pickle seed. "Listen, girl. 'Were you wanting extra help?' "

"Was you wantin' hextra 'elp?"

The crowd laughed again, and she yelled at them. "All right, you try it! You try it, if you're so clever, you stoopid hyenas!" She ran away, pursued by the same kind of empty cackling that would laugh at a drunken old woman, or a dog with a tin can tied to its tail.

In her narrow little room, with only Joey to listen, his bright head cocked intelligently and his eyes unwinking, Eliza practiced the question which would unlock all doors for her. When she thought it sounded perfect, just like Higgins, she took it along to a large flower shop in Euston Railway Station, where people coming into town for a spree bought buttonholes, and husbands on their way home from work bought bunches of flowers to sweeten up their waiting wives.

"Were yew wanting-gextra 'elp?"

They laughed at her. Like the thick-headed idiots in the Market, they laughed at her, and their laughter was even more unkind, because they had clean hair and clean clothes and clean hands and faces and should have known better.

Chapter 3

AFTER THIS, there was no more Professor Higgins to be seen in Covent Garden Market, with his long tweed coat and his quirky eyebrows and his eyes that saw a joke where no one else did, guessing, "Mile End Road" and "Hoxton," as easy as kiss your hand.

Eliza did not expect to see him again. He had finished with them and done, like a flower split open to see how the seeds formed, and then thrown in the gutter.

Christmas had come and gone, with nothing to mark it but the memory, grown dimmer each year, of her mother decorating a puny tree, and making a cloth animal for her, one each year. Eliza had kept them all, but when they moved to Euston Road, Mrs. Hardcastle had burned them in the kitchen stove, in case they carried bugs from Lisson Grove.

And then on Saturday night when they had been performing the opera *Götterdämmerung* (she recognized the thump of drums and all those shouting women from where she leaned against a lamppost outside the Opera House), Eliza saw him again.

"Buy a posy for your lady, sir?" She was just shoving her flower basket under the nose of one of those pink-cheeked young simpletons with a bored girl on his arm wondering why she had gone to all that trouble with her dress and hair to spend an evening with *this*, when she saw him.

Henry Higgins came out of the Opera House with the chattering crowd, elegant in evening dress, with a black cape and an ebony cane, and a silk top hat which he clapped at a dashing slant onto the side of his head.

"How much the v-v-v-violets?" Before the pink-cheeked young man could stutter it out, Eliza had turned her back on him, and slipped through the crowd.

"Flower for your buttonhole, Professor?"

Higgins was with a friend, a tubby, middle-aged man with a plump rosy skin that ran right up his cheerful face and over the top of his bald head, and a piece of glass stuck in one eye like a window on the world.

"And so I tried to show her, my dear Pickering —" As Eliza bumped her basket into the diamond studs on his white waistcoat, the professor said, "Speak of the devil! Here she is. Miss Lisson Grove in person. I never thought I'd see you still street peddling. Didn't you get the job?"

"Don't be funny." She scowled down into her basket. "They laughed at me."

"Didn't you say what I taught you?" In his swallow-tailed coat and his tall silk hat, he seemed yards above her. "What did you say?"

She repeated what she had said in the flower shop at Euston Station, and Henry Higgins, rot and blast his soul, laughed at her too, standing there outside the Opera House, with all the nibs and nobs looking in sideways surprise at him, and the duchesses raising their lorgnettes.

"Don't laugh at the poor girl, Higgins." The tubby man caught his arm. "Come on, or we'll never get a taxi."

"I just want you to hear her talk. She's so deliciously, hopelessly, incurably the crude voice of London."

Tubby tried to pull him toward the street, but Higgins drew him back against the poster of a huge Wagnerian lady on the wall, pushing Eliza in front of them.

"Wait, Pickering. Just listen to her a minute. Part of your education. This is Colonel Pickering, my dear. He's an expert on Sanskrit," he said seriously, as if she could understand what he was talking about. "He's come all the way from India to work with me on a book about nineteenth-century international vowel sounds. Isn't that exciting?"

"You're making fun of me again."

"*Agyne*. You see, Pickering, how they murder the language?"

"Leave her alone. It's not her fault. After all, she's never had anyone like you to teach her." Although the colonel seemed a kinder man than Higgins, he was a bit toady, as if he were trying to flatter the professor. Perhaps Higgins *was* someone famous after all, though Eliza doubted it, after the way the duchesses with the lorgnettes had looked at him.

"That's true," said Higgins, accepting the flattery. "I'll bet you I could take a girl like this — any girl, right out of the gutter — and in six months I could teach her to talk like a lady. Pass her off anywhere in society."

"Ha, ha, ha!" The piece of glass in his eye fell out as the colonel threw back his bald pink head and laughed, long horse teeth gleaming yellow. "You're quite a comedian, aren't you, my dear chap?" He replaced the monocle. "Now that you've had your joke let's go on home. There was some talk of Napoleon brandy, if I . . ."

"No taxis about . . . fine night . . . walk it . . ."

Eliza hardly heard what they said as they moved away. There was an excited ringing in her ears, and an idea was charging about in her mind like a horse trying to get out of a stable.

Keeping close to walls and railings, slipping across open spaces like a phantom, Eliza followed them, their long shadows thrown ahead as they passed a lamppost, thrown behind by the next lamp, and then forward again as they passed it. It was a long walk. Up Charing Cross Road, along Oxford Street, then cutting through the hushed impressive squares where only one family lived in each pillared mansion, and into a long street where footsteps seemed to fall more softly, as if in awe of the expensive elegance of the tall terrace houses.

Eliza had never been this way before. She marked the name on a corner sign, Wimpole Street, and hung back as the professor, stepping jauntily, and the colonel, slightly puffed, turned up a set of black-and-white marble steps and went inside. When the heavy double door shut behind them, she nipped forward and saw the number on the arched fanlight above the door. 27a. 27a Wimpole Street. A light came on in an upstairs window, and she caught a glimpse of Higgins, rubbing his hands as he went toward the fireplace, before a pudgy woman's hand drew the velvet curtains across and shut Eliza out.

Mrs. Hardcastle always went to church on Sundays, sitting bolt upright in a stiff guardsman's coat buttoned high on the neck and a black tricorn hat, with eyes aimed like rifles at the pulpit, daring the minister to tell her something she did not know already.

So the next morning, with the landlady at church, and Alfred Doolittle asleep on his back and snoring, Eliza went down to Mrs. Hardcastle's ground-floor rooms and borrowed her spring hat with the cabbage roses and her ostrich feather boa. The hat was too big. It spun round on her head if she turned too quickly. The feather boa, which was shedding a bit, like the old dog it was, tickled her nose and made her eyes water. But she felt quite posh enough for any 'Enry 'Iggins, as she retraced her steps along the quiet Sunday pavements to 27a Wimpole Street.

She had rehearsed what she would say. When a butler opened the door — a butler! She hadn't reckoned with a butler! — she said: "I want to see Professor 'Iggins. I 'ave some property of 'is."

"I'll take it." The butler, who looked like a worried monkey with gray side whiskers, not all that alarming, reached out, but Eliza held on to the leather glove which had once clothed the left hand of the late Mr. Hardcastle.

"I'll give it 'im meself."

"I'm sorry, miss, I really can't allow —"

"And *I'm* sorry, but I can't allow either. That makes two of us."

Although the butler was dressed in a black jacket and striped trousers, and spoke in accents most refined, she recognized, underneath the clothes and the accent and the silvery whiskers, a fellow cockney Londoner like herself, come up in the world.

"I'll thank you to remove yourself, my girl." He wasn't as tall as she.

"And I'll thank you to get out of my way before I —"

"What's all the shouting? Shut that door, Nutterville, there's an infernal draft." From the top of the stairs, in a Paisley silk dressing gown with a tasseled sash, Professor Higgins frowned down at them. "What's going on down there?"

"It's this young person, sir. She —"

"Good Lord, it's Lisson Grove. What the devil —"

"It seems she picked up your glove, sir."

"Bring her up, bring her up. I say, Pickering, this is extraordinary," he called over his shoulder. "Here's your education again, paying us a formal call. What a joke."

No joke, my lad, thought Eliza, as she plodded up the red stair carpet. She was shown into a large warm room full of deep chairs and rugs and desks and lamps and strange machinery, and books and books and books. All the books in the world on these walls. Where did he put the wallpaper? She stood in the middle of a deep carpet, with her toes turned in and her jaw set.

"Hullo! What are you doing here?" From the depths of a chair in the corner, Colonel Pickering arose, like a monster from the sea.

Eliza turned too fast, and had to straighten her hat.

"That's not my glove, anyway," said Higgins.

"I know it's not," Eliza said pertly, as the door shut behind the monkey butler. "It was just an excuse to get in. I want to ask you something."

"You've got a nerve." Higgins dropped into a chair, legs crossed, hands dangling, as if her boldness had exhausted him. "Go away." He closed his eyes. "You're bringing on a headache."

"Let's hear her anyway." The colonel came forward and took her arm. "Sit down, my dear. Don't be nervous."

"I ain't." Eliza sat on the edge of the chintzy sofa, tossing back the end of the feather boa, which kept rising up and threatening to choke her.

"Come on, come on." Higgins spoke with his eyes closed. "We haven't got all day. I'm busy."

"Well, this is business," Eliza said, "so I ain't wasting your time. In fact, I'm bringing you a stroke of good fortune, though I say it meself."

"Get on, girl. Get on with it."

"Well, you know what you said down the market that day when all the blokes and them was there, and you was guessing where they was borned, and that? Hoxton, Selsey, 'Eyegit 'Ill . . ."

"Highgate Hill," he corrected automatically.

"You told 'em you give lessons, didn't you, in speaking right? Well, you've got a new customer. I've come for me first lesson."

"You must be mad." Higgins opened his eyes and sat upright, uncrossing his legs. "I wouldn't dream of it."

"I can pay, if that's what you mean," Eliza said sharply. For months she had been saving for a warm coat, hiding pennies and sixpences in a paper bag under her pillow where Mrs. Hardcastle could not claim them for rent, nor her father wheedle them out of her for beer.

"How much do you think I get for giving private speech lessons?" he asked, amused.

"I don't know." She looked round the room, at the comfortable furniture, the long brown velvet curtains, the cushions, the rugs, the leather-bound books, the complicated machinery of great cylinders and trumpets that must cost a lot, whatever it was for. "But I've got almost seven bob saved. Now that's a lot of money, mind."

Higgins laughed, but the colonel said, "It's a lot to her."

"I don't care if it's a fortune," Higgins said irritably. "The girl is out of her mind, and I won't listen to any more of her nonsense." He reached behind him and pressed a bell on the wall.

"Out of me mind, am I? Well, I've got ears

just the same. Was *you* out of your mind last night when you said to this 'ere gent with the glass eye, 'I could take a girl like that and teach 'er to talk like a lidy'?"

"By Jove, you did, you know, Higgins." The colonel nodded.

"What if I did? Can't a man even think out loud without every Tom-Dick-and-Harry riff-raff of the streets taking him up on it?"

He looked across the room at Eliza. The hat with the roses was wobbling over one eye. Her hair was coming down. She had a bit of ostrich feather up her nose and was wiping it away with her sleeve. "And yet, you know," he said thoughtfully, "it would be a bit of a lark. This hopeless guttersnipe . . . what a test of my skill."

"Look here, I'll lay you a bet!" The colonel's face and the dome of his head flushed red. His monocle fell out again and dangled on its chain against his round stomach. "If you can make this poor girl into a lady, if you can pass her off in society at some grand affair like an Embassy ball, I'll pay all the expenses of it. Your fees for lessons, dance instruction, deportment, clothes, furs, jewels, whatever she'd need."

"By George, it's tempting."

"You rang, sir?" The butler opened the door.

"A mistake." He flapped a hand without looking at him, and the butler went out, with a critical glance at Eliza on the sofa, as if he were thinking the cover would have to be washed after she left.

"If you can do it" — the colonel looked as if he were going to have apoplexy — "you'll be the greatest teacher in the world, and I'll shout it from the rooftops!"

"*Could* it be done?"

"By you, it could."

As they talked excitedly across her, Eliza turned her head from one side to the other, the hat rocking like a boat in a rough sea.

"I'll do it! I'll take your bet!"

"Done!" They stood up and clasped hands.

Eliza jumped up too. " 'Ere, 'ere," she said. "You've forgot one little detail, gents." They turned in surprise, as if a grub had come out of the rose on her hat and spoken up.

"You've forgot to ask me."

"It's all settled."

"Not by me, it ain't." Ooh, he was a conceited devil. "I've got ideas of me own and feelings too, much as it may surprise you. Well . . ." She smiled from one to the other. of them, making them wait, feeling her power. "Maybe I will, and maybe I won't."

"Oh, shut up." Higgins pricked the bubble of her power. "Don't try to be coy with me. I don't like women. I learned years ago to stay clear of them, so don't expect me to treat you like a girl, or to notice how you look, or flirt with you or any rot like that."

" 'Ow dare you!" Eliza tossed back the

boa with an air. "If you was the last man on earth —"

"Though she isn't as bad looking as all that, actually," the colonel said, screwing in his monocle, "under the dirt."

"Thanks for nothing," Eliza growled, but Professor Higgins said cheerfully, "Soon get that off!" He went to the fireplace and picked up a tube like a snake that hung from the wall.

"What's that?" Eliza asked suspiciously. She had heard about the new-fangled invention of a machine to suck up dirt.

"Speaking tube." He put his lips to it and blew. In a moment, a hollow crackle could be faintly heard, as if there were a prisoner in a dungeon miles below.

"Ask Mrs. Pearce to come up here, would you?" Higgins said, and put the stopper back in the end of the tube. "She'll fix you," he told Eliza.

"I'm off." She got up and went toward the door.

"No, no, you idiot." The professor was a man of many faces, depending on whether he was getting his own way. He pouted now, like a spoiled child. "You're not going to ruin everything, and make me lose the bet, and spoil all my fun." He got between her and the door. "Listen, you ungrateful creature. I'm offering you far more than you've ever had in the whole of your miserable life.

I'm offering you clothes, jewels, cars, ball gowns, the perfumes of the East, champagne and chocolates, rich young earls who will swoon at your feet. . . ."

"Get out!" Now she knew he was insane. "Me?"

"Yes, you, girl. You want to be a lady. You said so."

"I never —"

"Yes, you did. You want to talk right, so you can go anywhere and they won't laugh at you, don't you?"

"I might get that job in the flower shop?" She looked up at him, and saw that his pout had changed to the eager smile that was so catching you had to smile back, however uncertain you felt.

"You might. You might indeed. You shall!" He grabbed her grubby hands as if he were going to swing her off the ground.

The door opened, and a plump elderly lady with iron gray hair in a round loaf on the top of her head and hands folded under the front of her billowing apron stood there regarding him severely.

He dropped Eliza's hands, and rubbed the palms of his own together, as if he had been gardening.

"Take her away, Mrs. Pearce, and clean her up. Give her a bath. Wash her hair. Throw away those clothes, or burn them. Find her something she can wear until we get her some decent things."

"You'll pardon me," said Mrs. Pearce, "but I've been your housekeeper for ten years, Professor Higgins, and given satisfaction, I hope, and I think I'm entitled to ask for an explanation."

"It's like this, Mrs. Pearce," the colonel said soothingly. It was obviously his part in life to step in and smooth down the rough spots raised by the ruthlessness of people like Higgins. "The professor and I have a new project. We're going to — er, help this nice young girl to make something of herself."

Mrs. Pearce stared at Eliza without comment.

"In short, we're going to make a lady of her. Won't that be fun?"

"You'll never do it," and "Fun for who?" said Mrs. Pearce and Eliza at the same time, and glared at each other.

"Oh, yes, we will. With your help." He was a great old flatterer, the colonel was. "Six months, that's all it's going to take, and then we'll pass her off in the highest society."

"And then what, may I ask?"

"Oh —" said Higgins vaguely, "that's her affair. Don't be such a wet blanket, Mrs. Pearce."

"If it's not too dampening to your spirits, Professor, may I enquire what is her name?"

"Oh, I don't know. Call her anything you like. Jane. Gertie. Ermintrude."

"My name's Miss Eliza Doolittle, and don't you forget it."

"Doolittle." The professor dropped his chin into his hand in thought. "Yes, well I daresay we can do something with that."

"I still don't quite understand, sir." She understood all right, the old battle-axe, but didn't want to. "You mean you're actually going to take this young person into the house, and, as it were, remould her?"

"Precisely. Like a sculptor." Higgins made shaping movements with his hands. "Now take her along, there's a good Mrs. Pearce, and find her a room and fix her up. I don't want to see her again until she's clean."

"I don't like to speak out of turn," said Mrs. Pearce, although she was obviously in the habit of saying what she liked when she liked in this household, "but you can't just pick people up like pebbles, Professor. This young Miss — Miss —"

"Doolittle," muttered Eliza, who was beginning to feel depressed by all the talk.

"She must belong to someone. What about your father, girl?"

"Oh, 'e won't care. I'm in 'is way really, and 'e in mine. Sometimes I wish it was 'im and not me mum who died. Does that sound wicked?" She turned to the professor, because Mrs. Pearce would be sure to say yes.

"Not at all. There have been times when I've wished I'd been born an orphan," Higgins said, unsmiling. You never quite knew whether he was joking or not. Even Colonel Pickering did not always know. That was why he said, "Ha, ha, ha" nervously, and dropped his monocle.

Mrs. Pearce heaved a great sigh, which swelled her apron front to an alarming size. "Come along then, Eliza." She jerked her head toward the door. "We'll have to see what we can do."

"Oh no." Eliza clutched the feather boa, as if she were going to be stripped right there on the carpet. "I'm going 'ome. I've got to — got to kiss me dad good-bye."

She had not kissed Alfred Doolittle for years, but she was not going to move in here without her bird Joey, that was one thing sure.

"How do we know you'll come back?" Higgins narrowed his eyes at her.

"I'll leave you me valuable furs. 'Ere you are." She unwound Mrs. Hardcastle's moulting feather boa and handed it haughtily to Mrs. Pearce, who looked as if she had been handed a bad fish.

Nutterville, the butler, was summoned to show Eliza out. At the front door, he said, "Shall I call my lady's carriage?" and made a rude noise with his lips.

"I'll be coming to live 'ere, my good man," Eliza said. "So watch your manners."

Out on the pavement, walking in a kind of a dream toward Euston Road, she suddenly realized that although the professor and the colonel had got the whole thing fixed up, she had never actually told them "Yes."

Chapter 4

BACK AT THE HOUSE in Euston Road, Eliza dropped Mrs. Hardcastle's big rose-garden hat over the railing into the basement dustbin, where the old girl could find it when she went poking to see if anyone had thrown food out, and think what she liked.

The kitchen door was open and when the landlady heard Eliza come in, she called out, "You're two hours late for dinner, so don't come whining to me, my girl."

Eliza went into the kitchen. "I couldn't touch a thing," she said grandly, although even the word dinner made the juices come into her mouth. As she left 27a Wimpole Street, she had smelt roasting meat and potatoes baking in their jackets and the sweet spicy perfume of apple pie, and almost fainted from desire, right there on the checkerboard tiles of the front hall.

"Is the old man in?" If he was, she was going to tiptoe past his door and get away without telling him where she was going. She owed him nothing. She wanted nothing from him. He wouldn't miss her. If Higgins or the colonel gave her any money, she might send him some, and he would be glad that she had gone "to a better world," as the preachers said, though they didn't mean Wimpole Street.

"The old man?" Mrs. Hardcastle shook her black helmet of hair carefully, so it wouldn't come down. "He's gone off with that crowd of boozers. Somebody's birthday they're going to celebrate. We'll not see him for three days at least, and nor will the corporation dustcart. I tell you straight, Eliza, if he gets the push, it's out. Hardcastle by name, but not by heart, but I won't be put upon, and if he goes, you go too, and good riddance."

"Oh, don't bother about me," Eliza said. "I'm off anyway. I shan't trouble you no more with me unwelcome company. I'm moving in with friends."

"Hoity toity," said Mrs. Hardcastle, obviously thrown off balance. For the first time, Eliza was glad of the professor, rude and conceited and unfeeling as he was. Glad of the pink tubby colonel. Glad for the butler and Mrs. Pearce, because of where they lived.

Standing in Mrs. Hardcastle's cold smelly kitchen with the tube train rumbling below like an uneasy stomach, and a pan of rancid fat congealed on the black iron stove, and the padlocked food cupboard, and the picture of Mrs. Hardcastle's bulldog mother on the dresser, she had a vision of that upstairs room at Wimpole Street, with the fire and the carpet and the soft lights and the deep chairs and the smell of chrysanthemums and expensive pipe tobacco.

"Does your dad know you're going?"

"Oh, yes," lied Eliza.

"He didn't tell me." Mrs. Hardcastle could not stand anything to happen, even a fire ten streets away, and not be the first to hear of it. "He knows you owe me money, I suppose."

"What for?"

Mrs. Hardcastle thought quickly. "Your share in this month's coal."

Eliza laughed, right in her face, for if there had been any fires in that house she had felt the heat of none of them. "Here's my new address then," she said. "27a Wimpole Street. You can send me the bill."

And see if I'll pay, she thought, running up the stairs, whistling to Joey.

The bird and the cage and the sailor hat and the paper bag of money were all she took. She had nothing else.

Arriving back at Wimpole Street in a taxi,

she met the colonel on the front steps, and asked him to pay the fare.

"My word, you're learning fast," he said admiringly. "I believe we shall make a lady of you yet."

Mrs. Pearce gave a short squawk when she saw the bird cage, but it turned out that the butler liked birds, if only to spite Mrs. Pearce. The butler and the housekeeper, Eliza soon began to see, waged a kind of underground cold warfare. As housekeeper, Mrs. Pearce thought herself head of the household, and let no one forget it. So as she said, "The bird goes out," Nutterville said, "He shall hang in the sunny window in the butler's pantry," and bore him off, chirping merrily.

Mrs. Pearce pushed Eliza up the back stairs, pinching her arm to relieve her feelings.

"I'm not going to let you meet the rest of the domestic staff before you've had a bath." She took Eliza into a huge bathroom with a tub that had feet like iron claws, and a brass geyser that coughed and rattled and let off a cloud of steam like a locomotive when she turned the knobs.

"A bath? I don't want a bath. I 'ad one last month." A bath was something you took two or three times a winter in the public bathhouses, mostly to get warm.

"Take off your clothes," Mrs. Pearce said grimly. Eliza didn't think she was going to like her. She had a motherly shape and a round pudgy face like a muffin, but there was nothing else cosy about her.

"And catch me death of cold? Not I."

"You'll have to get used to it." Mrs. Pearce began to undo the buttons on Eliza's coat. "Ladies bathe every day."

" 'Struth," said Eliza. "I don't want to be a lady then."

"But a lady you shall be," Mrs. Pearce said firmly, several times in the course of scrubbing Eliza, washing her hair and tying it back in a thick wet horsetail and fitting her out in a plain pinafore dress that belonged to the housemaid. "A lady you shall be, if it kills us all. As well it may," she said, planting Eliza in front of a mirror, and standing back with folded arms to see what she thought of herself. "As well it may."

"Blimey," Eliza said, peering. "Is that me?"

"Blimey," said Mrs. Pearce, allowing herself a smile. "It is."

The girl who looked at Eliza out of the mirror had big dark eyes and thick dark hair, a pale skin, and a soft wide mouth that began to curve upward in delight.

" 'Ere," she said in wonder. "I ain't bad lookin'."

The dress was plain, but it showed that she had a neat figure, and with the old wrinkled black stockings off and on their way to the fire, the ankles and feet below the hem were small and — and — "pretty," she whispered, rising on her toes and trying a little dance step.

Mrs. Pearce soon put a stop to that with a pair of brown button boots.

"Whose room is this?" There was a chest of drawers, a little armchair, a dressing table, a bed with a flowered spread and three pillows.

"It's yours."

"Mine!"

"As long as you keep it clean and tidy," Mrs. Pearce said. "Otherwise you'll go down next to the coal hole." She jabbed a finger downward as if she were pointing to hell.

"Mine." There were flowered curtains at the window, and outside, the top branches of a tree, bare against the darkening sky. Three pillows! Eliza could have cried, but she wasn't going to let the old lady see that it was paradise.

From far below, a gong sounded up the back stairs. "Are you hungry?" Mrs. Pearce asked.

"Starving." It was so long since Eliza had eaten anything, she could not remember what it was. Oh yes, that pork pie she had shared with Billy last night before she went to catch the people coming out of the opera. Billy! What would he do? He was the only one she minded about.

"You'll take your meals with us in the servants' hall, of course."

"Of course." Eliza had no idea what a

servants' hall was. It turned out to be a long, comfortable room in the basement next to the great stone-floored kitchen, with easy chairs before the fire, and a long table set with a white cloth and blue-and-white plates and more knives and forks than anyone could need, unless they were going to steal them.

The butler and the women servants were sitting at the table. They stared at Eliza, and she stared back at them, feeling her face on fire.

"Here she is," Mrs. Pearce announced. "His lordship's new experiment."

Someone giggled, and she added sharply, "You'll treat her right, Mary Jane, and all the rest of you, or you'll get the back of my hand across your ear."

Eliza sat next to the girl who had giggled, a saucy country girl with pink cheeks and bright eyes like a robin. "Don't be afraid," she whispered. "She won't eat you."

"I could eat 'er," Eliza whispered back. "Or a 'orse, or anyfing." There was a piece of bread on her plate, and she had to clutch her hands in her lap to stop herself grabbing it and stuffing it into her mouth.

Mrs. Pearce was saying a long and haughty grace, as if she were doing God a favor, but at last the little kitchen maid came staggering in with a huge piece of meat. The butler took up a carving knife, and that was the end of talk, or even thought, for Eliza, as she filled the hungry gap of years.

She was too busy to copy the way the others ate. "Table manners will have to be her first lesson, Mr. Nutterville," Mrs. Pearce said, as the teapot came in, and Eliza sat back and blew out her cheeks, wondering if she would ever be able to get up.

The butler — he was called *Mr.* Nutterville down here, very polite, although the professor called him Nutterville, or Nutters — said, "If you want the others to treat her right, you'd better do the same yourself."

'Ear, 'ear, thought Eliza. He was going to be on her side. She sent him a wide smile down the table, and he grinned and winked at her and said, "Keep your chin up, mate," just like any of her friends in the market.

"What's that?" She jumped and spilled her tea, as a piercing whistle blew in the room.

"His highness." Mary Jane made a face.

Mr. Nutterville went to the speaking tube, which hung from the wall like the one in the professor's room, removed a whistle from the end of it and said in his refined, upstairs voice, "You blew, sir?"

The distant hollow voice said something, and the butler answered, "Very good, sir," and put the whistle back for its next deafening performance.

"He wants you upstairs, Miss Eliza." He pointed at the ceiling and made a solemn face.

She jumped up, and Mary Jane said, "Don't

get excited, dearie. He's not the answer to a maiden's prayer."

They all laughed, and Eliza thought, This is going to be a bit of all right. I shan't care how strict or rude them two are up there with their old lessons. We'll laugh about them down here and have more fun than they do.

The upstairs room was called the study. The fire was burning in a bright glow, and Higgins and Pickering were in such deep chairs that all she could see of them was their feet stuck out on the brass fender, a hand in one chair holding a glass of brandy, a hand in the other dangling a cigar.

"The young person, sir." Nutterville sent her into the room and shut the door behind her. He wasn't going to let his tea get cold, even if hers had to.

"Come here, Eliza. Don't stand there all night."

She walked across the carpet in her tight button boots, and stood on the bearskin rug before the fire. The professor and the colonel sat bolt upright as if she were the queen come to pay a surprise call.

"By Jove, you wouldn't know it was the same girl. When we get you some pretty clothes, you'll be a knockout," the colonel said, screwing the glass round and round in his eye to see more of her.

"Get away, you old goat," Eliza said. "I know your kind."

Higgins winced. "Seeing her spruced-up exterior, one forgets how vile she still is within. Say, 'Get away,' Eliza."

"Git awye."

"No, no. Get a-way."

"That's what I said."

"Tomorrow, we shall make some recordings of your voice. Then you'll be able to hear— if you can stand it — just what you sound like. Colonel Pickering and I have mapped out a program for you." He pointed to a large chart which hung on the wall behind the leather-topped desk. "Lessons begin at nine a.m. sharp." He pulled himself up out of the deep chair like a stork unfolding from a nest. "Come, I'll show you some of the apparatus."

One end of the room turned round a corner, and was lined on three sides with books. Below the books were shelves and tables and trestles and tripods, holding all kinds of strange machinery, with wires and needles and trumpets and snaking tubes, and a weighted stick that raced madly back and forth — tick, tock, tick, tock — when she put out a finger to it.

" 'Ere." She sucked her finger. "What you goin' to do — torture me?"

"If you work hard and do what you're told," Higgins said, "there won't be any torture. Except to me," he added, making the screwed-up pickle face again, as Eliza said,

"Coo, you ain't arf a rum geezer, guv'ner, straight you ain't."

He stopped the tick-tock machine. "That's a metronome, which is used to get perfect timing. It will also help you with your piano practice."

"Pianner! You didn't say nothing about pianner."

"All part of a young lady's cultural education," the colonel said. He got up and went over to the little piano that stood against a wall, with nymphs and shepherdesses painted on its graceful front. "Let's test your musical ear." He played a few bars. "What's that?"

"Ow, shut up. If you think I don't know 'Gawd Save the King' — "

"It happens to be Elgar's *Pomp and Circumstance.*"

"She'll come to it, Pickering. Don't rush her. After all, there wouldn't be any point to the bet if she weren't the most ignorant cabbagehead that ever came out of the back slums of nowhere. Excuse me." He bowed. "Lisson Grove. Here's the recording machine, Eliza. The very latest model. You talk into this little receiver here, and that makes the needle print on this wax cylinder as it goes round, and — hey presto! — your voice will come out of this big green horn, just as if you were inside the box."

"I never!" Eliza forgot how annoying he was, because the machine was so fascinating. "You mean I could reely 'ear meself?"

"You may regret it. Try something."

"All right. Anything for a lark. Like me to give you a song?"

The professor turned a knob, the cylinder began to roll, and Eliza clasped her hands in front of the pinafore dress which felt so strangely stiff and clean, leaned forward to the receiver and sang one of the songs from the bad old days at the shirt factory.

My old man said, "Foller the van,
And don't dillydally on the wye."
Off went the van wiv me 'ome packed in it.
I followed on wiv me ol' cock linnet.
But I dillied and dallied,
Dallied and dillied,
Lost me wye and don't know where to roam — oh,
You can't trust a special like an old time copper,
When you can't find your wye 'ome!

"By George, I like that!" The colonel struck a couple of chords on the piano. "How does it go?" He picked up the tune as she sang it again, and they ended up singing together.

Oh, you can't trust a special like an old time copper,
When you can't find your wye 'ome!

"By Jove, Eliza, we'd make a fortune on the music halls." The colonel beamed at her, and mopped his shiny pink forehead with a great colored handkerchief.

Eliza was flushed and happy, but the professor clicked off the machine, and said, "You'd better get to bed."

"Ain't I going to 'ear me luverly voice?"

"Tomorrow, perhaps, if you're a good girl. Remember, nine o'clock sharp, I said. If you're late, you will get no lunch."

Outside on the landing at the top of the stairs, Eliza did something she was to do many many times before the six months were up. She turned and stuck out her tongue as far as it would go at the oak-paneled door of Professor Higgins' study.

Chapter 5

"Now, just once more, Eliza. Say your vowels, and try to get it right this time."

"I know me vowels."

"Say them."

"Eye. E. Oi. Ow. Yew."

"Listen to me. A — E — I — O —U. Doesn't that sound better?"

"Luverly," said Eliza. "Eye. E. Oi. Ow. Yew."

"Now, Eliza," said Higgins patiently, although his mouth was a straight line and you could almost smell the sulphurous volcano smouldering within. "You wouldn't want me to give up in the very first week, would you?"

"At this rate, I wouldn't give a blow. This

is much more boring than what we ever done at school. We used to draw pickshers there, and say pomes and that."

"All right." Higgins got up from his seat across the desk from where she sat in a hard straight chair, day after day, moving her mouth to match his, trying to copy the gibberish sounds he made. Vowels! Whoever invented them, she'd gladly strangle him. "All right. We'll recite some poetry, if that's what you like. What's your favorite?"

Eliza thought back into the dark mists of her schooldays in the little classroom with cracked windows stuffed up with newspaper, and mice running over your feet after the sandwich crumbs.

"Baa baa, black sheep?" she offered.

"I'm not familiar with that." It was hard to imagine that Higgins had ever been a child. He was born in long tweed trousers and a sporty yellow waistcoat with a chain across it for the turnip watch with which he timed the lessons of unfortunate flower girls.

" 'Ow about Good King What's-'is-name?"

"I think we'll save that for next Christmas. I don't feel strong enough for it now." The professor went over to the bookcase and reached up for a book. He was tall enough to reach books on the top shelves, but the colonel had to climb up and down a little stepladder. The ladder was fun. Eliza climbed it when she got the chance, and sat on the top step with her long navy serge skirt wrapped round her legs, looking out through the window at the well-bred life of Wimpole Street: the cars and chauffeurs, and the uniformed nannies with pampered babies, and the dolled-up ladies and gents with their little toy dogs and their little toy children, who looked much too neat and clean to be real.

But she wasn't there for fun, as the professor reminded her twenty times a day, so he always said, "Get down. Ladies don't sit on stepladders."

And when she sat on the chair by the desk, the colonel would fuss at her. "Don't sprawl. Ladies keep their backs straight and their ankles crossed and their hands in their laps."

"I hate ladies." She had decided that in the first two days. She was never going to be one, not if they kept her here for a hundred years, making her open her mouth and put her lips just so and her tongue just so, and say them rotten vowels.

"Here we are. Alfred Lord Tennyson." He put an open book into her hands.

"One of the nobs, eh? I didn't know lords 'ad to work for a living."

"People like Tennyson don't think of writing poetry as work."

"It is, though."

"How do you know? Have you ever written any?" That dancing, eager sparkle leaped into Higgins' brown eyes.

"Get away. I mean, that putting words down on paper, that's a lot of work. Me dad wrote a letter once, and it took 'im three days. Nearly killed 'im."

A few tears came into the back of her eyes at the thought of her father. She had wanted to get away from him, but it was insulting that he had not even tried to get her back.

"Read here." His eyes had gone chilly and severe again. "Say it after me: *Come into the garden, Maud, For the black bat, Night, has flown.*"

"*Come inter the garding, Maw-aw-awd.* Coo, 'e was a touch fresh, wasn't 'e?"

Higgins continued, "*Come into the garden, Maud, I am here at the gate alone.*"

"Well, she didn't expect 'im to bring all 'is friends, did she? *Come inter the garding, Maud* — oh, cripes!" She threw the book away and collapsed in giggles, her hands over her eyes. "I can't say that stuff, guv'nor. It's too bloody daft."

Mary Jane, who was the parlormaid, came in with two cups of coffee and two Chelsea buns on a tray.

"Nothing for me?"

"Mrs. Pearce said you weren't to have nothing between meals," Mary Jane said primly, but as she passed close to Eliza's chair, she dropped a ginger cake into her lap.

Eliza crammed it into her mouth while the professor wasn't looking, and when he suddenly said, "Say your vowels!" she spluttered and choked and sprayed the carpet with crumbs.

"All right," he said, "if you insist on putting things into your mouth, we'll do the marbles again."

"Ow, not them marbles!" He was a torturer after all. Them blokes with the rack and thumbscrews, up at the Tower of London, they had nothing on him.

He took six marbles out of his pocket and put them in her mouth, and she sat there looking at him, her eyes and cheeks bulging.

"All right, we'll try nursery rhymes, since you're not ready for Tennyson. *London Bridge is falling down, falling down, falling down.* Let me hear each word, clear as a bell."

"La-da Bwa ith fawa da —" She looked up at him like a despairing spaniel, and the colonel grunted himself up out of his chair in the corner and said, "Don't be too hard on the girl, Higgins. I'm not sure it's legal."

Colonel Pickering could be almost as devilish as Higgins when he got carried away by teaching, but he was at least not insane, which Eliza was sure by now the professor was. "Come on, Eliza," he said, "we know it's difficult, but if you'll just try your best —"

"Don't slop over her," Higgins said sharply. "You don't train a dog by stroking it."

"I ain't a dog!" Eliza cried, and gave a shriek. "Gorblimey, I've swallered one!"

"That's all right," said Higgins comfortably, putting his hand in his pocket. "I've got plenty more."

He tried to make her mumble on about

London Bridge, until she was near tears. "It'th impoth —" She spat the marbles into her hand and dropped them in his coffee cup. "It's impossible. I ain't going to try no more."

"If Demosthenes could do it, you can."

"Who's 'e when 'e's at 'ome?"

"He was an ancient Greek who had almost as many problems as you — no breath, no enunciation — a complete disaster. But he trained himself to become a great speaker by shouting at the sea with his mouth full of pebbles."

"Yes," said the colonel gloomily, "and look what he came to in the end. Suicide."

"If you're not going to help, I wish you'd go away."

"And leave you with this wretched girl? No, sir."

"When's lunch?" Eliza asked.

"Not till you've done your breathing. The secret of all good speech is breath control, as I think I've told you."

"Only arf a duzzin times." She had to stand on a certain rose right in the middle of the carpet — the respiration rose, he called it — and not breathe in the ordinary way she had been breathing for eighteen years. Ho no, that was much too simple for his Lord High Mucking 'Iggins. She had to take a deep breath and hold it while she moved her stomach in and out like a cab horse with the heaves. Oh, it was sickening. And then he would hold a candle in front of her face and make her say, "Ha, ha, ha. 'As 'Arold 'ad hany 'urricanes hover in 'Ampshire?"

If she sounded the *h* properly, the candle flame would flicker. She did this for ten minutes by Higgins' watch, until she was dizzy from lack of breath, and if that 'Arold 'ad come 'ome from 'Ampshire, she would have slapped him right across 'is haggravating face.

By midday each day she was ready to run away and never come back. She could tell from the professor's face, let alone the sarcastic things he said to her, that she wasn't doing any better. She would never get it right. She would never be a lady. She would never get into the fairyland of the flower shop, and when the professor made her say those rotting vowels, "Just five more times before lunch," she knew she didn't care.

But when she staggered downstairs and fell into her place at the table in the servants' hall ("Sit up straight, Eliza, and have you washed your hands?"), not Higgins, nor Pickering, nor Mrs. Pearce, nor not being allowed to eat chicken drunsticks with your fingers could spoil the bliss of a three-course meal, with soup and meat and spuds and pudding, and often a hunk of cheese besides.

After lunch she knew she would stay, if only to see what there would be for dinner.

One day, when she had been in the house

for over a week, Nutterville went up to answer the front door bell at teatime, and came back dusting off the tips of his white gloves delicately.

"Her grace is honoring us with a visit."

"Blimey — a duchess?" Mrs. Pearce had been drilling Eliza in who was what among the titled personages she would meet when she was launched into society, "*if* that day should ever come," Mrs. Pearce always added, in case Eliza should fancy herself.

Nutterville laughed. "Only Mrs. Montgomery Higgins, mother of the great professor of that name."

"Well, someone had to be his mother, I suppose," Mary Jane said, and Eliza added, "Pore woman."

"Now, girls, I won't allow that sort of idle talk about the master," fussed Mrs. Pearce, although she allowed it all right if she was the one who started it. She got up. "I've a hundred things to do, even if no one else has." She never actually did anything but give orders, but her life's cry was that she was the only one in the house who did any work. "You girls get busy now. Eliza, help Mary Jane to clear the table." Eliza was not supposed to do any work with the servants, because she must spend all her time and energies at her lessons, but Mrs. Pearce, who did not approve of a common flower girl spending all that time upstairs with the master, was always finding jobs for her, "to keep her in her place."

As soon as all the others except Mary Jane had left the room, Eliza went to the speaking tube and put her ear to it so that she could hear what was going on upstairs.

"You haven't been near me for days, Henry, so I've come to see what you're up to, you shocking creature."

Talk about Demosthenes and pebbles in the mouth! Mrs. Higgins' throaty aristocratic voice sounded as if she had a head full of burned currants. "Blimey," Eliza whispered to Mary Jane, "am I going to sound like *that?*"

"I told you, Mother, Colonel Pickering and I have been very busy. We're working on a special project."

"What project, if I may be so inquisitive as to ask?"

"Well, it's — it's a bit of a secret at present. You'll know, of course, some day. The whole world will know."

"Do you think the whole world will be interested in nineteenth-century international vowel sounds?" She made it sound like manure.

"International — ? Oh, yes, the book. Yes, that's it. We're working on it night and day."

"Day and night," added Colonel Pickering solemnly, in case she was not convinced.

So! They were not going to tell Mother

about Eliza. She couldn't be trusted not to spill the beans, probably. Eliza imagined her, a talkative old lady in a hat trimmed with poor murdered birds, chattering gossip and scandal over the tea table.

"You ought to get out more, Henry. Be seen about at the right places. People think it very strange that my brilliant son never goes with me anywhere. Not that I care what they think, but you ought to be looking for some nice harmless girl with looks and money."

"I've got plenty."

"Yes, you've *made* money, in your own funny, famous way. But your father always used to say, don't you know, that inheriting money is so much less *vulgar* than earning it."

Eliza almost exploded with laughter, right into the tube, which would have blown the whistle in the study and shaken the old girl up.

"I'm rather nervous, Henry, of these — what I call *intelligent* — girls you meet at the university. Promise me, you'll never be tempted to marry one of those bluestocking creatures with thick legs and hair like a bird's nest."

"I'll never marry anyone, Mother," he said irritably. "There's no such thing as the kind of woman I —"

The door of the servants' hall opened, and Eliza dropped the tube quickly and picked up a pile of plates.

The lessons went on, even on Sundays, and Eliza grew more unhappy and Higgins grew more irritable. Even the colonel was depressed, although he looked like winning his bet.

"But I'd be glad to lose," he told her. "If you can be turned into a lady, like the toad, who became a Princess, I shan't care how much it costs me."

The only progress Eliza seemed to be making was that when the professor played his voice and hers back to her on the recording machine, she began to be able to see the difference.

But what of it? Just because he didn't talk like her, that didn't make him right and her wrong, any more than the Russians were wrong because they didn't speak English.

"I ain't so sure I want to talk like you anyway," she told him one day as he switched off another recording of that miserable Maud and her boy friend by the garden gate. "S'welp me, I ain't."

"So help me," he corrected. "I'm not."

"So 'elp me. S'welp me. I like mine better. What's wrong with the way I speak? All me friends talk like that, and there's nothing wrong with them. I'll kill the man who says there is. What's it matter 'ow people speak? What's the point of all this?" She waved a hand round at the study with its books and desks and dictionaries, which had once seemed like luxury but now seemed a prison. "What's the point of it all?"

"The point, my dear Miss Doolittle, is that English is a language of the greatest power and beauty, and you are murdering it with your ain't. Since cavemen first scratched on stones, poets have been clothing passionate ideas and trumpet calls of glory in the splendid garb of the English language. The noblest sentiments that ever flowed in the hearts of men are contained in its extraordinary, imaginative, and musical mixture of sounds. And you are massacring it with your s'welp me. Are you following me?"

"S'welp me no, I ain't."

The colonel knew a bit about birds, and they brought poor old Joey up from the butler's pantry, and taught him a few elegant phrases, if only to show that he could do better than Eliza.

"Good morning," he now said, instead of " 'ullo," and, "excuse my glove."

He hung in the window of the study and cheeped and whistled at the sparrows in the street, and said, "Excuse my glove, excuse my glove, excuse my glove," until the colonel threw a silk handkerchief over the cage to shut him up.

Higgins had brought in a long mirror on a stand, and Eliza had to stand in front of it by the hour, with her feet just so — one heel against the other instep, her hand clasped at her waist just so, and watch the movements of her lips and her pink tongue against her small white teeth.

"Eye, e, oi, ow, yew." In the mirror, she saw a girl in a long dark pleated skirt with big pockets and buttons, a starched white shirt and a broad black tie, which the colonel said made her look studious. He and Mrs. Pearce were in charge of clothes. Higgins didn't want to bother with that, though he was sharp enough if she came in with her cuffs unbuttoned or her hair untidy. In what she was beginning to think of as the dear old days of Euston Road, she had tied her hair with a shoelace and gathered it up all anyhow, with a few pins stuck in if she could find any. Now it was drawn smoothly back in two dark wings, falling shining behind her and tied with a big black bow.

It was still hard to get used to herself.

"Stop admiring yourself," the professor would snap. "You're there to watch your lip movements, not the thrilling beauty of your countenance."

He kept on at her and on at her and on at her, making her repeat over and over again the sounds which she could never hope to get right, and making her read endless passages from boring books she could not possibly understand.

Everyone except Higgins was sorry for her. Even Mrs. Pearce was not so hard on her now that she was not the professor's pet, but his victim. Eliza was miserable upstairs, but below stairs they played cards and told fortunes in teacups, and had many honest laughs at the expense of the helpless gentry who paid good money to servants for doing things they could have done themselves.

Mr. Nutterville, the butler, who had once been a steeplechase jockey, had taken to Eliza as if she were a daughter. She called him Uncle Nutters. He dropped the fancy talk now, and answered her back in her own cockney, and even went so far as to let her see that the dignified silvery side whiskers were stuck on with spirit gum.

He would take them off sometimes after supper and they would all have a glass of wine if he had managed to smuggle some down from the dining room, and Eliza and he would entertain with duets, of "Two Luverly Black Eyes" and,

> My Father's a gingerbread baker,
> My mother she fiddles for gin.
> My sister picks locks for a livin' —
> My Gawd 'ow the money rolls in!

Some evenings the bell would ring or the whistle shriek rudely from the wall, and it would be a summons for Eliza to go back upstairs to Higgins and Pickering while they had their brandy and cigars.

"Rot 'em," she said, but she had to go. In spite of all the rebellious talk, there was no mutiny in this house.

Sometimes it was lessons again, until she nearly dropped from exhaustion. Sometimes the colonel would go to the piano and she would sing. They were trying to take the foggy London harshness out of her voice and put sweetness in it.

They made her sing "Beautiful Dreamer," and "You Are the Honey, Honeysuckle, I Am the Bee," and "Cherry Ripe, Cherry Ripe," and other such soppy ballads. If she tried hard, she was allowed to let herself go into her own kind of song, and the nicest times they had up there, with the fire a flickering glow and the winter night shut out, was when she sang for them "Won't You Come 'Ome, Bill Bailey," and "My Old Man Said 'Foller the Van.' "

It was the only time the professor relaxed and enjoyed himself. You saw what he could be like if he was not possessed by this mania, like a drug or alcohol, to make a silk purse out of the sow's ear that was Eliza Doolittle.

One evening Uncle Nutters brought in the late post on a silver tray. There was a letter from America, which made the professor get up and pace the floor, long legs spanning half a dozen roses on the carpet at each stride.

"Moral Reform League," he fumed. "What do I care about moral reform, Eliza?"

"I dunno. I don't even know what a moral is, let alone reform it."

"Lucky girl. Morals is being told not to do what you want to do by someone who doesn't want to do it. Moral reform! Just because this Ezra D. Wallingford is a millionaire, he thinks he can get me to drop everything and go charging across the Atlantic to make a speech at his annual meeting. It's the third letter I've had. I can't stop the wretched man."

"Perhaps," suggested the colonel sensibly, "if you answered his letters, he might stop."

"Brilliant, Pickering, but I'm ahead of you. I'm already considering in my head the most insulting way of saying no. You shall write it, Eliza. That will be even more insulting."

Breathing hard, tongue between teeth, fingers cramped round the pen, Eliza painfully wrote out what Higgins told her. The lines ran crooked down the page, and there were blots and even holes where the nib had caught the paper.

"Splendid!" Higgins put it in an envelope and stamped it. "Run down to the corner right away and post it before I lose my nerve."

"The day you lose that," Eliza said, "I'll know you're perishin' well dead."

She put on her warm coat and ran down to the red pillar box on the corner of the street, hair flying behind in the crisp cold night. It felt so good to be out and free and young that she ran all the way round the block of houses, and came back to number 27a panting and glowing.

A man was standing on the doorstep with his finger on the bell. A man in a sagging leather jacket, a leather hat with a flap behind, and thick baggy trousers tied round the knee with string.

It was her father. Eliza was opening her mouth to say, " 'Ullo, Dad," when he stepped aside with unusual politeness and said, "Good evening, miss. Am I right for Professor 'Enry 'Iggins?"

He didn't recognize her! He didn't know his own daughter. Well, since he had not bothered whether she lived or died for three blooming weeks, she was not going to bother to tell him who she was.

Nutters opened the door, and Eliza went into the hall. "Tradesmen's entrance is round the back," he said as soon as he saw Alfred Doolittle.

"Not for me, it ain't," he said. "I've come to see me daughter, Eliza Doolittle, and find out what's goin' on 'ere."

Nutters, who was quite quick in the up-take, realized that he had not recognized Eliza and grinned.

"Bert Nutt!" Mr. Doolittle stepped through the doorway in his clumping dustman's boots and peered at the butler. "Strike me dead if it ain't Bert Nutt from the old crowd I used to meet at the Red Lion after the races. Ex-jockey, wasn't you? What are you doin' 'ere?"

"Pardon me." Nutterville drew back from the gust of the beer with which Alfred Doolittle had fueled himself before he came. "My

name is Horace Nutterville, and I am not ac-
quainted with the Red Lion or the Old
Crowd. I don't recall we've ever met."

"If he didn't recognize you," he told Eliza
as they went down the basement stairs after
he had taken her father up to the study, "I'll
be blowed if I'll let on I recognized him."

Eliza went straight to the servants' hall
and picked up the speaking tube. This should
be something to hear! If Higgins had been
annoyed over that millionaire, thousands of
miles away in America, what would he say
to her father on the carpet on his study,
smelling of beer and garbage?

She heard her father's voice, faint at first,
and then louder and all too familiar, hoarse
and jovial, as he came nearer the fireplace.
He told them that he had got the address
from the landlady. "I would 'ave come before,
of course, to see me beloved daughter, the
pride of me 'eart, but I've been away on
business."

He must have taken off his leather hat, because the professor said, with his usual rude-
ness. "There are only two places where they
give you a haircut like that. Prison and the
army."

"Take your pick, guv'ner," said Doolittle
cheerfully.

So that's where he'd been! He'd been in
jug before, without caring too much, because
the company was good and the food regular.

"Now listen here," Eliza heard her father

say, in the bullying tone that always pushed into his voice when he'd been on the beer, "I don't want no jokes. I've come on very serious business."

"Born in Hounslow," Higgins jumped in, as if he were playing Snap. "Mother Welsh, I think. Father — could be a dash of Lancashire somewhere in his family?"

"None of your business, mister, Where's my daughter?"

"Is that any of your business — now?"

"She's my daughter. She's under twenty-one. The law's the law. She belongs to me."

Eliza's heart was beating excitedly. It was thrilling to hear them going at it in a tug of war over her. Like in the olden days when knights fought duels over fair maidens.

Well, not quite.

"All right." Higgins suddenly let go of the tug rope before he'd even start pulling. "If you want her, take her."

"Wait a minute. You got me wrong, guv'ner. I'm not sayin' you can't have her. I just want to know, where do I come in?"

"The law," said Higgins, at his most chilly, "is most certainly the law, as you so brilliantly put it. One of the things it's very firm about is blackmail."

"Blackmail!" she could imagine her father putting on his saintly bishop's face, dustman's hat held over his heart, outraged to be so accused.

"If you sent her here in order to get money

from me, you miserable man, you can take
her away this minute, before I knock your
teeth out."

"Two can play that game," Doolittle said.
"I could take me fists to you for blackening
me good name."

The professor suddenly gave a shout of
laughter, and her father laughed too. What
was going wrong? Why weren't they fighting
over her?

"Well, I mean, we're all friends 'ere, and if
you want the girl, I'll let you have her, but
if I mention that I don't think it should be
for nothing, I don't want you jumping down
me throat again with Blackmail. Because it
ain't."

"What is it then?"

"It's like this. You want Eliza, the devil
knows why. I don't want 'er, and the devil
knows why that is too. Look at it this way. If
a pub keeper 'ad a pint of beer, and you were
thirsty and he wasn't — would 'e *give* it to
you?"

"He would not."

"There, you get the point. I knew you
would. I can tell a real gentleman when I
see one. And what's a five-pound note to you,
after all?"

"To — buy her?"

"Sort of on hire. If you want to buy 'er, I'd
'ave to ask fifty."

"You'd sell your daughter for fifty
pounds?" Even the professor was slightly

shocked, and Colonel Pickering said, "Have you no morals, man?"

"Can't afford 'em, guv. If Eliza's going to get a bit out of you, why not me too? Them what they call the deserving poor, widow women and that, they get all the charity. I'm just as poor, but if there's anything going and I put in for a bit of it, it's always the same story. You're not deserving, so you can't 'ave it. But I'm just as poor as a deserving widow. I don't need less. I need more, because I eat and drink more and expect to get more fun out of life. I put it to you gents, is it right for you to take advantage of me faults to do me out of the price of me own daughter what I've fed and clothed by the sweat of me brow? Would you grudge me five miserable pounds?"

Eliza smiled to herself. He'd never take them in with that slippery line of talk. But Higgins said, and sounded serious, "You know, Pickering, this chap is so gloriously double-tongued, we could make him a politician or a preacher in three months. It's not so much that he has no morals. He's got *new* morals. Do you think we ought to give him a fiver?"

"He'll only make bad use —" the colonel began, but Doolittle interrupted. "Not me. I need it desperate. I'm behind on me rent, see, and if I can't pay up, there's only one way out. I'm going to have to marry me land-lady, Mrs. Hardcastle by name. Prunella

Hardcastle. Prune and prism, I call 'er. Mrs. Hard-as-nails, Flintcastle. She's got me trapped. But with five pounds I could pay what I owe and keep me freedom. Take 'er on a spree, perhaps, keep 'er sweetened up, but not marry 'er."

"You know," the professor said, "I like this man. He's so absolutely shameless, you've got to love him."

Oh, it was sickening! Eliza would have blown a raspberry up the tube if she had not wanted to hear more. He'd fooled them, as he had fooled everybody, from her mother on. "You've got to love him," people were always saying. Why?

Higgins must have handed over a five-pound note, for Alfred Doolittle said in the rich glowing voice that came from money in his pocket, "Eliza's all yours. If she don't behave, give 'er a lick of your belt. That's the way I brought 'er up, and look where it's got her — 27a Wimpole Street. Very classy. You must admit, five pounds isn't much return for all I done for 'er."

Higgins laughed. "Get rid of him, Pickering," he said helplessly, "before I give him ten. By gosh, Erza D. Wallington should hear his ideas. That would make them sit up at the Moral Reform League. I tell you what, let's write Erza D. another letter — I mean a real one, not an Eliza letter — and tell him he ought to send for Alfred Doolittle. A common dustman, but one of the most original moralists in England. We'll have a drink on that. Whiskey, my dear Doolittle?"

"Well, I don't normally touch a drop—" (Ooh, thought Eliza, may God forgive you. Or strike you dead.) — "but seeing as you've been so understanding . . ."

Eliza heard the clink of glasses. "Cheerio."

"Up your nose, guv'ner."

"All the best."

"Let's get Eliza up to see you," Higgins said, and before she could move away, a piercing whistle nearly blew her eardrum clear through her head and out the other side.

She stamped her foot, her eyes filling with tears of pain and rage. Whistle yourselves blue in the face, I won't go!

She ran up the back stairs, hand clapped over her ear, which was buzzing like a furious wasp, went into her room and bolted the door.

Some father! Sold his only daughter for five pounds! That Higgins was just as bad to give it to him, and there they were, drinking and laughing, as if they'd done something clever. "You've got to love him." Love him! They ought to shoot him. Some father!

She threw herself on the bed, and hot tears poured out onto the pretty flowered spread. "Oh, Mum — why did you have to go and die!"

Chapter 6

AFTER THAT, Eliza was so disgusted that she didn't care about anything.

Like a puppet, she dressed herself in the plain, school-girly dresses that Mrs. Pearce put out for her. Without even bothering to look in the mirror — for who cared whether she lived or died, let alone what she looked like? — she pulled back her hair in a thick braid or a swinging horsetail, or coiled it up in a bun, as Mrs. Pearce ordered.

She mouthed through her lessons with no interest and no improvement. She stood sullenly on the respiration rose and lifted her diaphragm obediently up and down in time to the tick of the metronome. She blew up balloons to help her lung control, but no longer bothered to burst them in the professor's face, as she used to. Even when she was allowed to move on to a new verse of "Maud," it was all the same to her.

> Birds in the 'Igh 'All garding,
> When twoiloit was fallin,'
> "Mawd, Mawd, Mawd, Mawd,"
> They was crying and callin'.

"High Hall garden," Higgins corrected for the umpteenth time. He lit that dratted candle, and set it on the desk in front of her. "High Hall garden. Say that twenty times and blow out the flame."

" 'Igh 'All garding. 'Igh 'All garding," Eliza repeated tonelessly. She was almost as disgusted with Higgins as with her father. "A great character. Salt of the earth," he told her. "If I had him to teach, instead of you . . ."

He thought Alfred Doolittle was a rare and lovable joke.

Well, you can 'ave 'im, 'Iggins. The two of them were a fine pair, for they were both dead selfish, and neither of them had any idea that anyone else had any feelings.

Quite blind to her wretchedness, driving her like a slave to get what he wanted, Higgins was working her harder than ever, and losing patience more quickly. There had not been much fun before, but now there was none at all. There was no more singing "My Old Man," and Eliza would not have sung it if he asked her.

He had moved her over to his swivel chair on the other side of the desk, so that she could turn north, south, east, and west, and throw her voice to all corners of the room. He would take one vowel sound at a time, and keep on and on at it, until she was ready to scream, or kill herself. Or him.

There was a long paper knife on the desk, shaped like a dagger. Once she picked it up and looked at the point, as Higgins was saying, "Let me hear it once more. 'The rain in Spain stays mainly in the plain.'"

"The rine in Spine stys minely in the pline." At each hated vowel sound, Eliza jabbed the point of the paperknife viciously into the red leather top of the desk.

"Wishing that desk was me?" Higgins asked serenely.

She glowered, gripping the handle of the dagger.

"But don't forget, girl, your daddy has sold you. I'm all you've got now."

Eliza burst into tears of rage and exhaustion.

"Oh, for heaven's sake! If you're going to blubber like a baby —"

Colonel Pickering, who was a kindly old soul, but no use at controlling Higgins, came and patted her shoulder nervously, as if she were a dog and he had never had a dog, and said, "Dash it all, Higgins. The girl does have some feelings, after all."

"There's no time for feelings," Higgins

said. "Here's over a month gone by, and she still can't tell me where the rain falls in Spain."

The servants were all against him now, and on Eliza's side. Often he would make her work right through a mealtime, and sometimes he sent her to bed without any supper, for things like losing her temper and swiveling the chair round so violently that the seat came right off its screw and landed on the carpet with her still in it. Then Uncle Nutters would send her up a chicken leg and a glass of wine, or Mary Jane would creep up the back stairs with cups of tea and buns, and they would picnic on her bed in the dark, so that old hawkeye Higgins should not spot the light shining into the back garden.

One wet January day, when he had tried to make her sing "God Save the King" with her mouth full of marbles, she ran away.

She put on her double-breasted coat with the big brass buttons and the pockets like huge envelopes, bundled her hair up out of the rain under her green turban, and went back to the dingy house in Euston Road.

"Take me back, Dad," she was going to say, but he was out, and so was Mrs. Hardcastle. One of the lodgers let her in, and she climbed up through the stale food smells which hung about the bare familiar stairs.

Her tiny slot of a room at the top of the

house was open. So Old Hardbitten had never been able to find a lodger desperate enough to take it. The mattress was gone, and Eliza climbed over the rusty bed springs, and knelt to look through the grime on the window at the wet gray landscape of slate roofs and blackened chimney pots.

Kneeling there on that sagging iron bed, with the springs cutting into her flesh, and the dirty peeling walls closing in on her like a coffin, she thought of her bedroom at 27a Wimpole Street: white painted furniture, flowered curtains, and the sparrows in the lime tree waiting for her to bring crumbs for the window sill.

The cracked bell on the Church of St. Appollinaris struck three o'clock through the sooty rain. "Can't . . . turn . . . back," it said flatly.

Eliza scrambled back over the bed, and ran down the stairs and banged the door behind her, as if she wanted to shut the hateful house up forever. Her coat and the bottom of her long skirt were dirty already just from being in the place ten minutes. Mrs. Pearce would flay her alive. When she saw dirt, she screamed as if she had seen a mouse.

Threading her way with remembered ease among the cars and horses and trundling open buses of Euston Road, Eliza walked down the long street she had trodden so many times in her draggled skirts and her leaky cracked boots, and went in among the cobbled archways of Covent Market, looking for Billy.

She had forgotten that she was not dressed right for the market. Some of the porters whistled at her, and one cried, "Oh, I say!" in a fancy voice.

She saw Billy before he saw her. He was sheltering under an archway, leaning against a pillar with his hands in his pockets and his coat collar turned up, his hair plastered over his forehead like wet straw, his blue eyes looking vacantly at nothing. He often stood like that, not thinking, not seeing. Not asleep, but not quite awake either, like a horse in a stall.

She came right up to him, and he looked at her blankly. He didn't recognize her, until she said softly, " 'Ullo, Bill, me old mate."

"Blimey—" His jaw dropped like a ton weight. "Eliza!"

"Don't know me with me face washed, eh?"

He nodded and shook his head and smiled and frowned and blinked and stared all at the same time, totally at a loss. He took his hands out of his pockets, reached to put them round her, and drew them back, gasping and stuttering and treading on his own feet.

Eliza put her hands on her hips and laughed. "Well, you 'aven't changed, that's for sure," she said. " 'Ow do you like me duds?" She twirled, showing off her clothes, and minced a few steps over the wet cobbles, like the ladies she could see parading when she sat on the stepladder in the study in Wimpole Street.

She thought he would tell her that she was luverly, or at least be quite impressed by the change in her. But when he got enough control of his breath and his tongue and his wits to speak, all he said was, "Well, we'll soon get them things off you, old girl," as if she was covered with ants or cobwebs.

"You missed me, Bill?"

She hoped he would tell her that he had not looked at another girl, but Billy didn't look at girls anyway. He was scared of them, so it was no compliment, even if he had stayed faithful. Flummoxed by her question, he cleared his throat hoarsely and spat among the sodden cabbage leaves in the gutter. "Going to take the barrer down to Caledonian Market," he said. "Get old Gertie to lend you a shawl or something, and you can come on down with me. See if we can sell some of them Brussels sprouts."

"Brussels sprouts! Your old chum comes back to see you after all this time, and all you can talk about is Brussels sprouts. Crikey, Bill, ain't you got no soul?"

"I dunno," he said blankly. "But I do know I got to get rid of them sprouts before they rot on me."

Can't . . . turn . . . back. The words

beat in Eliza's head as she trudged away through the darkening streets. She had enough money in her pocket to take a cab, but she wanted the dark, and the bright streaks of rain across the gas lamps, and the evening noises of the city. Feet hurrying home on the wet pavements, the clop of the bearded horses pulling the empty coal wagon home over the wood paving blocks, the swish of bus wheels through the muddy gutters, carrying people home.

Everyone was going home. It was time for her to go too.

She had thought Professor Higgins would be angry because she had run away, but he had not even noticed her rebellion. He merely said that since she had chosen to take the afternoon off, she would have to work later than usual that night.

She changed her wet clothes and ate some supper, and refused to answer the questions in the servants' hall about where had she been and what had she done and why had she gone out without telling anyone.

"I thought you had gone for good," Mary Jane said, through a mouthful of suet pudding. " 'We'll never see *her* again,' I said to Mr. Nutterville. 'She's gone and I don't blame her.' Why did you come back, you soppy thing?"

"Oh, shut up your noise," Eliza said. "I'm tired." No use trying to explain to them what she had found out. *You can't turn back.* They wouldn't understand.

The professor was harder on her than ever that night. Perhaps he did know that she had tried to run away? They worked on and on, while the colonel fell asleep before the dwindling fire, and the clock on the mantelpiece chimed the quarters and the hours, and Mrs. Pearce came in, fussing like a hen, and said that it was past midnight and everybody ought to be in bed.

"No one is going to bed," Henry snapped, "until someone can speak like a human being instead of a savage. I'm not even asking her to speak like a lady any more," he said bitterly. "Just like a human being."

"You'll make the girl ill," Mrs. Pearce said smugly as she went out, as if it would be worth doing, to prove her right.

"I'm ill already." Eliza put her head in her hands. "I've got a headache and a throat ache and a backache, and me feet is killing me."

"You shouldn't go walking all afternoon in the rain. Rain. Rain." He snapped his fingers, as if she were a trick seal.

"Rine, rine," she said, without looking up.

"The rain in Spain stays mainly in the plain."

"The rine in Spine stys minely in the pline."

"You think you've got a headache! The

top of my head is opening and shutting like a door. Every time it opens your hideous vowel sounds come in like a caterwauling tom-cat."

"I don't care."

"Look, Eliza Doolittle." He dropped his long body into the opposite chair, and flung his hands out on the desk. "This is your last chance. Bet or no bet, I can't go on much longer. This is your last chance to be a lady. Don't you *want* to go to the Embassy ball in a golden coach with six white horses and a prince to kiss your hand? Don't you *want* to sit in a velvet box at the opera with diamonds round your lily-white throat and in your shining hair, and all the duchesses peering up at you through their lorgnettes and asking, 'Who is she?' Don't you *want* to have a satin gown with a long train and three feathers on your head and go to Buckingham Palace and meet the King?"

"And if I ever did," Eliza said, jutting out her jaw at him and narrowing her eyes, "you know what I'd say?"

"The rine in Spine stys minely in the pline, I suppose. He'd love that."

"I'd say, 'You can arrest 'Enry 'Iggins, Your Majesty. You can lock 'im up because I say so, and if you like you can cut off 'is 'ead, and 'e can cry all 'e wants for mercy, before and after it's off, but all I'll do is cheer, be-cause I'll be glad — glad — glad!" Flushed and angry, half sobbing, she glared at him across the desk.

But he would never rise to a fight. That was the most maddening thing of all. "The rain," he droned, with his eyes closed, "in Spain . . . stays mainly . . ."

All of a sudden, as Eliza sat there with her hair tumbling down and tears staining her cheeks and her eyes swimming with hopeless hatred for this cruel, pig-headed tyrant, she took a deep sobbing breath and said, very clearly, "The rain in Spain stays mainly in the plain."

"Who said that?" He did not open his eyes.

"I did." Eliza was as surprised as he was.

"Say it again."

He slowly opened his eyes, like a man reluctant to wake from a dream, as Eliza found her voice repeating, "The rain in Spain stays —"

Higgins gave a shout that woke the colonel with such a shock that he leaped out of his chair, waving an imaginary sword and yelling "Charge!"

After that, it was pandemonium. Eliza laughed and cried and laughed, and swiveled the chair round and round with her heels in the air, shrieking, "Come into the garden, Maud!" for all of a sudden, she could say that too.

The professor grabbed her hands and swung her off the chair and into a capering waltz, while Colonel Pickering, letting out cries of "View halloo!" from his old days in the hunting field, dashed to the piano and crashed out triumphant music.

"Excuse - my - glove - excuse - my - glove - excuse - my - glove!   Liza-Liza-Liza —"   She twitched the cover off Joey's cage, and he joined hysterically in the excitement, reeling off all the words he knew and some he never knew before, and dashing his beak along the bars of his cage like a demented harpist.

The tall oak doors of the study opened, and there stood Mrs. Pearce and Nutters. She was bundled in a dressing gown like next week's laundry, with her hair in a skimpy pigtail tied with tape. He wore a long brown hairy robe like a monk, with his silver whiskers stuck on crooked.

"What's up, sir?" he cried. "Is it a fire?"

Mrs. Pearce said, "What on earth is going on here?" and set her jaw as severely as she could without her teeth.

"She's got it! She got it right. Rejoice with us, for this day has been won a great victory!" The professor advanced on her with such a lunatic grin that she reeled back against Nutterville, and clutched the billows of cloth where her heart was supposed to be.

While the colonel thumped on the piano fit to wake the whole lower end of Wimpole Street, Higgins seized Mrs. Pearce round the middle, and Eliza seized Uncle Nutters, and

they twirled round in a crazy dance, with the
butler tripping over his long monk's robe,
and the housekeeper gasping, "Let me go!
Stop, stop! It will be the ruin of my blood
pressure!"

It seemed to Eliza that she had never been
so happy in her life. Half an hour ago, she
had not cared two farthings how she talked,
nor what became of her. But suddenly now
she could do it. Her headache had vanished.
She felt strong as a lion and light as a butter-
fly, and she knew how that man felt who flew
to the sun. His wings had melted though, but
hers wouldn't. She could go anywhere, do
anything.

"She even looks different," Higgins said
wonderingly. He had poured champagne for
them all to celebrate, and she raised her glass
to him, her eyes dancing and sparkling over
the bubbling sparkles in the glass. "By Jove,
Pickering, I feel marvelous. I feel like Pygmalion. Your health, Galatea!" He clinked
glasses with Eliza.

"Same to you. With knobs on, if I knew
who she was."

"Galatea was the ivory statue Pygmalion
carved, and the goddess of love brought it to
life for him."

"And then he married her," put in the
colonel.

"Bedtime," said Higgins abruptly. "The
party's over. Bedtime, everybody."

Chapter 7

WHEN Eliza awoke the next morning, with the sun pouring onto her face, she could not remember at first why she was happy.

Then it all came back to her. "The rain in Spain," she said out loud. "Birds in the H-igh H-all garden. 'Enry 'Iggins. H-enry H-iggins. Darling Henry Higgins!"

This was a gala day. She got up late, and the cook made her a special breakfast, with sausage and fried tomatoes, for the word of her triumph had blazed round, and the others were as pleased as if she had won the Derby.

She was relaxing in the servants' hall, with her feet on the fender, the steam from her third cup of tea caressing her nose, and the sounds of everyone else at work about the house soothing her ears, when a furious blast from the speaking tube sent her bolt upright, with tea all over her skirt.

"Where the devil are you?" cackled Higgins' voice when she picked up the tube. "You're forty minutes late."

"What for?"

"Lessons, of course."

"Lessons? I thought we were going to take the day off."

"Think again. We've only just begun."

Darling 'Enry 'Iggins. I don't think.

"H-enry H-iggins." The candle flame in the study flickered flat every time she brought out an aitch.

"H-as H-arold h-ad h-any h-urricanes h-over in H-ampshire? Ain't I doing well?" Lessons were not half as bad now that it was coming right. But he was no easier than before.

"Terrible. Has Harold had *any* hurricanes?"

"Ho, yus."

"Oh, yes."

If anything, he was even harder than before, now that he was off full-tilt toward his goal of bringing her out into society as a lady. But Eliza could stand it now, because she was beginning to succeed. She could hear on the recording machine that she was beginning to sound like a lady (*me!*), and it was all so exciting that sometimes up in her room she stood before the mirror and asked herself solemnly, "Eliza Doolittle, is this really you?"

The Embassy ball which would decide who won the bet was about four months away. That seemed too long to Eliza, who felt she could go to Buckingham Palace next week, and no questions asked. But Higgins worried. "It will be a miracle if we bring it off, with so much yet to cram in. Tone, pitch, rhythm, vocabulary, phrasing, dancing . . . etiquette . . . Make a list, Pickering. We've got to plan our campaign. Deportment . . ."

"My dad had a mate who was deported. Tony Gambello. Suspicion of foul play. I don't want no deportment. I'm doing fine 'ere." She glanced at Higgins. "Here."

"No, no. Deportment is — sort of behavior, and all that." The colonel waved his pencil vaguely. "Walking about with a book on your head. How to sit down and stand up."

"How to drink me tea?" Eliza asked as a joke, but the professor said, "That's right. How to drink your tea. Your table manners are still revolting. We'll have to see that Mrs. Pearce is more strict. When you have learned that a dining table is not a pig trough, you'll take your meals with us, and we shall drill you." He made delicate knife-and-fork and drinking gestures, and Eliza said, "Blimey, I'll starve to death."

"Deportment," went on Higgins. "Singing . . . world affairs . . . a few phrases of conversational French she can drop in here and there."

"I won't learn French," Eliza said, "and that's flat. I'm having enough trouble learning English."

"Eliza," said Higgins in the weary voice with which he warned her she was trying him too far, "there are approximately two thousand, seven hundred and ninety-six spoken languages in the world. If you are not a good girl, I shall make you learn every one of them."

The cold winds of March warmed into April, and a rainy April dried away into a sunlit May, with the scent of stocks and gilly-flowers rising from the walled back garden, and the lime tree thick with green outside Eliza's bedroom window. When she walked with the colonel in Regent's Park, as she did most afternoons to trim her ankles and freshen up her complexion, the crab-apple tree blossoms dropped soundlessly onto the bright turf, and all the women in London seemed to be dressed like flowers.

In other years, in the drab streets where her life was set, the coming of spring had meant only that she could be warm again. The birds and blossoms were celebrating elsewhere, and the women she knew had merely taken off a layer or two of jackets and shawls, and pinned a crumpled flower on the winter's headgear. But the women among whom Eliza now walked cast off their furs and put on peacock colors. Their huge swooping hats changed from velvet with feathers to straw with flowers. There was a whole garden on some of them, with sprays of osprey nodding among the foliage, as the white socks of their sailor-suited children flashed ahead after their hoops.

May blossomed into June, and Eliza and the colonel walked among the roses, pronouncing their romantic names, "Damask, White Royal, Maiden's Blush," and conversing carefully of this and that.

"How do you do?" the colonel would say politely.

"H-ow do you do?" It had taken her a long time to overcome " 'Ow dee do?"

"May I introduce Her Grace the Duchess of Overdone?"

"Charmed, I'm sure." Eliza bent her head with a gracious smile, and an elderly gent passing by squared his shoulders and put up a finger to spruce the ends of his bristling white moustache.

"What a charming gown, my dear," Colonel Pickering said in a high falsetto, playing the Duchess of Overdone.

"Thank yew — excuse me — thank you, your grace. I'm very flattered."

"Where do you buy your beautiful clothes, my dear?"

"Whiteley's," said Eliza, with a great puff of breath, managing to sound both the *w* and the *h,* which was a great feat. "When can we go to Whiteley's, Colonel Pick?" She slipped back into cockney, as she still did when she spoke quickly.

"How do you take your tea, my —"

He hastily dropped her arm and the falsetto voice, as a slender young man in a gray suit and elegant black-and-white shoes raised his straw boater and said: "Good afternoon, Colonel. Lovely day for a stroll, what?"

"What, what?" The colonel was flustered. "Oh — er — hullo, Freddy. Yes, yes. For a stroll, as you say. Ha, ha, ha."

The young man had stepped forward expectantly, looking at Eliza, but the colonel said, "You must excuse us. We have a train to catch," as if anyone would be strolling among the rose beds on their way to a train, and hurried Eliza ahead and round the corner of a hedge, leaving the elegant young man gaping.

"Where's the fire?" Eliza wanted to know.

"I can't have you meeting people yet. You're not ready. It would spoil everything."

"He looked a bit of all right though. I ain't spoken to a young man for weeks. I'm getting sick of never speaking to nobody."

"Anybody."

"Who was he?"

"Young Freddy Eynsford-Hill. His mother is a great friend of the professor's mother. If those two women got hold of this, it would be all over London long before July."

"I thought the ball was in August."

"It is, but you're doing so well, my dear,

that we're thinking we might give you a little tryout at some social event."

"And go to Whiteleys?" She plucked disgustedly at the plain brown-and-white dress which Mrs. Pearce had chosen for her to greet the summer. "And get me some pretty dresses? Oh, Colonel Pick, when?"

"Soon." He took her arm again after glancing round to see that the straw boater was not following. "We'll buy you some dresses and — perhaps we might take you to Ascot."

"To Ascot?" It was the most fashionable race meeting of the season. Even Eliza knew that.

"The professor thinks it might be a good idea to give you a trial gallop. He wants you to meet his mother."

"Why didn't he tell me?"

"He doesn't want you to get carried away and stop working."

"Fat chance. When he gets to hell, that man, he'll put Old Nick himself to work, and all the little demons will have to write in copybooks with their pitchforks."

But although Higgins still drove her like a galley slave, the lessons were not torture any more. Every day she made a new recording on the machine, and every day she could hear her own voice changing: softer, clearer, more musical. Sometimes they played one of the early recordings, of Eliza saying things like, "Come inter the garding, Mawd, Oi am 'ere at the gite alowen." She could laugh at it with them, although if they had laughed when she said it, all those weeks ago, she would have kicked them in the shins.

She was learning so quickly now that the professor was moved to say, "You know, Pickering, I begin to suspect this girl might have some intelligence after all."

"I'm a genius, I am."

"No, I am. The sculptor is the artist, not the statue."

Intelligence. That was a word that had no more been used in the old life than fish knives. Now it might be hers. Using her brain was an adventure, like using a limb that had once been crippled. She began to take books off the crowded shelves without being told to. Crouched in the window seat, with the cries of the strawberry seller in the street below, she read:

> The red rose cries, "She is near, she is near";
> And the white rose weeps, "She is late";
> The larkspur listens, "I hear, I hear";
> And the lily whispers, "I wait."

and she realized, with a shock of surprise, that she was actually reading Tennyson for pleasure. It was as if a key had been turned in a lock and opened a door to a flood of bright knowledge and understanding that cleared away the mists that had shrouded her mind.

"Dinner is served, sir."

"Come along, Eliza," Higgins said. "You

are going to take your meals in the dining room with us now."

"I'd rather be downstairs with all my friends, thank you very much," she said, with the new politeness that was growing on her like moss.

"Ladies don't eat in the servants' hall."

"Then I don't want to be a lady."

"That's a remark I seem to have heard before," Higgins sighed. "You explain to her, Pickering, there's a good chap."

"Well, you see, Eliza, it's like this." The colonel ran a finger nervously round between his high collar and his fat red neck. "They are your friends, of course, but it won't do — well, you can't — I mean, it's different, understand?"

"No."

"Well, in society, you see . . . Oh, dear, how can I explain?"

Nutterville, who had been standing by the door, listening with interest said, "Perhaps I can help. Listen here, Eliza, it's like this. The gentry is the gentry, and the servants is the servants. Right?"

"What am I?"

"If you eat in the dining room, you're the gentry. Got it?"

Eliza nodded, and followed Higgins and Pickering meekly to the dining room.

"You'll be too grand to talk to the likes of us," Mary Jane teased her afterward, and Mrs. Pearce said, "Tuppence to speak to you now, I suppose," and added, "if you forget to wipe your mouth like I taught you, you'll get the back of my hand across your ear." But Eliza still sneaked downstairs as often as she could, and drank tea and gossiped and played cards in the servants' hall, and sang duets with Uncle Nutters with his whiskers off.

She still had not met the professor's mother. She was always smuggled away if Mrs. Higgins came to call, in case she said the wrong thing, or dropped an aitch, or dipped cake in her tea. Mrs. Higgins did not come often, because she had been well-trained by her son, who trained people as other men train animals, not to bother him when he was busy.

Now they were going to take Eliza to Mrs. Higgins' private box at the Ascot race meeting.

"We'll surprise her."

"Surprise her with Eliza. By George —" The colonel's monocle fell out. "I made a poem! What shall she be? Your niece?"

"How could I have a niece without Mother knowing it?"

"I could be *your* niece, Colonel Pick."

"I've got no brothers or sisters."

"She'll be just a girl we know," Higgins said shortly. "Don't make problems. We've got enough of those already."

The first was the choosing of the dress. Ladies always dressed to kill at Ascot, and Eliza must be the most deadly of all. They could not ask advice of any of the women they knew, because the professor would not trust a woman with any secret, let alone the tremendous secret of the transformation of Eliza Doolittle.

Mrs. Pearce, puckering up her mouth like a dressmaker holding pins, advised, "Something frilly and flowered, with little scarfy bits here and there. Beading, lace, very à la mode."

"I want something simple. Stunningly simple. Something that will make the other women look like cart horses decked out for the costermongers' Easter parade."

"Something simple," he told the saleswoman in the model gown department at Whiteleys, the biggest store in London. "Something young, but not girlish. Plain, but not ordinary. You know what I mean?" He looked up at her with his face screwed up and one eyebrow raised.

He and the colonel were perching on little gilded chairs, looking as uncomfortable as bulls at a garden party.

"Is it for this young lady, sir?" The saleswoman was long and flat and clad from ankle to chin in black, with a dead-white disapproving face above.

"Well, it's not for me," Higgins said rudely. Like a trapped beast, he looked round the elegant salon with its mirrors and gold paint and die-away mannequins wandering among the silks and laces like lost souls.

"I'll see what we can find for your wife."

"She's not my wife."

"Oh, excuse me. Your fiancée. Charming," said the saleswoman, not looking charmed at all. She snapped her bony fingers at one of the fade-away girls, and said, "Model the turquoise taffeta, Miss Rosalie, if you please."

Eliza thought the turquoise taffeta was luverly, and also the primrose moiré silk, and the polka-dot organza, as the mannequins paraded blank-faced before them in one gown after another. The idea of wearing any one of those gorgeous dresses made her heart flutter under her starched white blouse; but the professor kept saying, "No," and "No, that's not it," and groaning, "Take it away," as Miss Ermintrude minced out in a raspberries-and-cream confection of ruffles and floating flounces.

The colonel was too busy staring at the girls to say anything at all. The saleswoman was getting sick of it. She shifted her feet as if her corns bothered her. "There *is* another Ascot gown," she said, "a black-and-white lace that was made for poor Lady Mary Fortescue, but then she . . . oh, but you wouldn't want it."

"Why not?" The professor sat up straight and stopped yawning.

"It's *very* expensive."

"How much?"

When she named the price, the colonel whistled. "That's far too much." But Higgins said, "Who cares? You'll have to pay for it when I win the bet. Show us the dress and stop haggling," he said irritably to the saleswoman.

It was the most beautiful dress Eliza had ever seen. A sheath of ice-white lace slashed with black and white ribbon, which hobbled her in below the knees fashionably, like a horse. The long skirt kicked out into a train (Gorblimey, she thought, what price the Covent Garden cobblestones on a wet day?), and the collar frothed up round her chin as if her face were precious china packed in tissue paper.

To go with it they bought a parasol like a white chiffon cloud, and a huge swooping chocolate-and-vanilla cake of a hat, with more feathers and plumes and bows than Eliza's head could possibly support.

"Hold your head *up*," commanded the saleswoman, taking more interest now that she had made a firm sale, as Eliza began to shake and giggle under the astonishing hat. "It isn't supposed to be comfortable. Keep your neck stiff, miss."

"All day?"

"Forever, if necessary. *Il faut souffrir, mademoiselle* — one must suffer," she translated, to Eliza's blank look, "in order to be beautiful." And allowed herself a smile, to go with the best she could do in the way of a compliment.

On the morning of the races, Mary Jane, who had once been a lady's maid, helped Eliza to put up her hair, cinched her into the dress, and fixed the great hat to her head with ornamental hatpins as long as meat skewers. Eliza took her ruffled parasol and hobbled insecurely downstairs to show herself to her friends in the basement.

"Oh, Eliza!" The kitchenmaid shrieked and threw her apron over her head. The cook was speechless. Uncle Nutters grinned his monkey grin and told her she was a real little topper, and Mrs. Pearce cried, she actually cried, did Mrs. Pearce, to see her ugly duckling become a swan.

"Eliza! Confound that girl — Eliza!" Higgins was ringing bells and calling all over the house. She came up the back stairs, daintily holding her skirt. "The car's here. We're late. What the devil are you doing down there, you blasted idiot?"

"You mind your tongue, mister," Eliza said, waving her parasol, "or I'll bash you one in the guts wiv me umberelly."

"If you talk cockney today, even as a joke," he said through closed lips, "if you say any ghastly word like 'guts,' so help me, I'll kick you out into the gutter where I found you."

"If you do," Eliza blew him a light kiss to calm his nerves, "you'll lose the bet and have to pay for this dress."

He was nervous. All the way down in the car, with the traffic of limousines and landaus

and busloads of gaudy race-goers thickening
as they crossed the river at Staines on the
Ascot Road, he fussed and fidgeted. It made
Eliza feel very powerful. He had staked so
much on her.

For the first time in her young life she was
the center of attention. She sat up straight,
her neck rigid "forever," as the saleswoman
had commanded, and a cool aristocratic smile
on lips that wanted to laugh and sing. People
stared and peered at her as they passed.
Would they think she was poor Lady Mary
Fortescue, because of the dress? She was Miss
Elizabeth Doolittle, only daughter of a retired
East Indian rubber planter and his invalid
wife, living quietly and respectably in Northumberland, and she hoped her profile did
not show that she had never ridden in a car
before and was practically taking flight from
excitement.

At the racecourse, all eyes were on her as
she and the colonel strolled over the grass
toward the grandstand. The professor had
marched on ahead, like a man forgetting his
dog. She had to take tiny steps on account of
the bow round her knees, "Like the string
round me dad's working trousers," she suddenly thought, and clapped a gloved hand to
her mouth to smother a giggle.

The professor, who despised conventions
and fashions, was wearing his usual tweeds,
but the colonel was decked out in full Ascot
rig: gray frock coat and trousers, silk cravat,

gray top hat, a carnation in his buttonhole. She was very proud of him.

"And I of you, my dear." They passed below the row of private boxes facing the racecourse above the heads of the colorful crowd. "That's Mrs. Higgins." The colonel jerked his head and spoke out of the side of his mouth. "In the hat like a winged muffin. Remember — say nothing except what we rehearsed."

Mrs. Higgins already had her race glasses focused downward on them. When Eliza came into the box on the colonel's arm, she glided forward as if on wheels in a way Eliza would have to copy if she was going to get about much in these here hobble skirts, and cried: "So there she is, Henry! Wherever have you been keeping her all this time, you wretched boy? She's beautiful!"

Eliza blushed, and turned her head away, because her deportment teacher, a prim old maid who had never been a girl, had told her that ladies did not blush unless a gentleman made advances.

"Her parents are retired, Mother, I told you. Up in the North." He had chosen Northumberland because it was the farthest place he could think of, and nobody who was anybody ever went there. "They don't get about much. Elizabeth has been hardly anywhere."

"Well, we'll soon put that right," his mother said delightedly. "She must go *everywhere*, a lovely girl like her." She held out a hand,

and Eliza took it limply and muttered something, keeping her lips stiff to stop them trembling. She was suddenly paralyzed with shyness, not because Mrs. Higgins was an alarming old battle-axe, but because she was much younger and prettier and nicer than she had imagined when she had eavesdropped on her through the speaking tube.

"Er — she's, well — she's — er, rather shy, Mother." (If you're going to get rattled too, Higgins, that'll cook me goose.)

"Nonsense, a lovely girl like her. Come, my dear. I'll introduce you to everyone."

There was a small crowd of people in the box, the men in gray suits and toppers, and the women in a dazzling rainbow assortment of flowers and frills and tassels and waterfall feathers that made Eliza glad of her dramatic black and white.

She managed to say, "How do you do" to everybody without missing a single aitch, but when she got to the last gentleman — "And this is Mrs. Eynsford-Hill's son, Freddy" — she opened her mouth without bringing out any sound, because it was the young man who had goggled at her in Regent's Park.

He was goggling now, and also bringing forth no sound. Love at first sight! They read about it in the twopenny novelettes in the servants' hall. *This* would be something to tell Mary Jane!

"Do sit down, Miss Er —" Freddy Eynsford-Hill, who had good looks, but could never lift a hundredweight of potatoes, if you got him in the market, found his tongue and a chair. "Haven't we met before? Were you at the Haliburton's ball last week?"

"I don't think so," Eliza had the wits to say. "But I go to so many I lose count."

"I heard Professor Higgins say you've hardly been anywhere."

"He doesn't know *everywhere* I go." Eliza sat on the edge of the chair, crossing her ankles as taught, and nodded at Higgins. One up to me.

"Get you some champers. Half a mo." Freddy spoke mostly in half words and half sentences, to conserve what little energy a life of exhausting idleness had left him.

"Let the others do the talking," Higgins had told her. But Freddy, who seemed to have more beauty than brains, merely stared at her as she juggled a glass of champagne and a plate of strawberries. His mother was watching them, and so was Mrs. Higgins, the two queens of gossip. They would class her a mute idiot if she didn't say something, and when they classed someone, Higgins said, it was all round London. So she took a deep drink of champagne and said carefully, "What delightful weather."

If there was no sun, she was to say, "What disappointing weather." Good thing she hadn't got them mixed, and mucked it up.

"Oh, rather," Freddy said as admiringly as

if she had made up a whole poem and re-
cited it.

"Do you enjoy the races?" There was not
a horse in sight yet, but that was her number
two sentence.

"Oh, terrif." He beamed at her as if she
had asked, "Do you think I'm pretty?"

He did think so. No one had ever looked at
her like that, with his heart in his soft brown
eyes. "What do you do?" she asked, forgetting her practiced sentences, but really wanting to know.

"Do?" He looked puzzled. "Oh — er, nothing really. What is there *to* do?"

"I mean work, and that. A job."

"A job?" He looked as if he were going to
faint or vomit, perhaps both. "I live with my
mother."

"Blimey, do you let your old lady support
you, a great big boy like you?" Eliza spoke
slowly, watching her vowel sounds like dan-
gerous criminals. "You" escaped as "yew," but
Freddy drowned it with a bray of laughter.

"I say, Miss Doo, you do make ripping
jokes!"

The other people stopped talking to hear
what the ripping joke was, and Higgins came
over and stood behind her chair, with one
hand in the small of her back, as if she were
his doll to wind up.

"I only said, 'Blimey, do you —'"

Higgins poked her sharply in the back.

"Let me get you some more champagne, Miss Elizabeth." He bent forward and hissed, "What have you said?"

"Quite all right, thank you, Professor Higgins." She smiled sweetly up at him, drained her champagne and handed him the glass as if he was her slave, instead of she his.

She was quite all right. She was doing all right, she was. Eliza Doolittle, late of Euston Road, up here with all the swells and nobs, with one toff in a topper looking at her as if she was Cleopatra, and holding her own as if born to the job.

By the time the races started, she had drunk three glasses of champagne and had forgotten that she had ever been anyone else but Miss Elizabeth Doolittle, the best dressed lady at Ascot. She talked more than she had been told to. "Because of the booze," she whispered to the colonel, when he muttered to her, "Steady," and "Whoa there," as if she were one of the racehorses who swept round the track at intervals, with nobody paying much attention to them.

She was doing all right though. They would never regret the price of this dress. When she started on another glass of champagne and said, "I 'ope the bubbles don't come back down me nose," Higgins explained it away as, "The new slang. All the girls talk like that."

"In Northumberland?" asked Mrs. Eynsford-Hill, who was a grim hulk of a woman with a nose like the prow of a ship and a hat in full sail.

"She's been in London quite a while."

"She's not one of your bluestocking students at the university?" the professor's mother asked in her amused voice, as if she had a private joke. "She doesn't seem to be the intellectual type."

"Don't worry," Eliza said cheerfully. "I ain't."

Freddy chuckled. "Oh, I say, that new slang's topping. Do teach it to me."

"I aren't." Eliza corrected herself a little sulkily. All of a sudden, he looked less handsome and more stupid. The champagne and the races and the whole of society was going a little sour. She'd had better times by far at the Epsom Derby, with beer and jellied eels, and all the blokes and Nellies kicking up their heels to the blind gypsy's accordion. If this was all there was to being a lady, they could have it. "Don't you ever bet on a race?" she asked Freddy. "My father would have a fit if he knew I went to a race and didn't back nothing. Anything."

"I didn't think girls were allowed to place bets," Freddy said.

"They aren't," put in his mother.

"There's a good horse called Dover in the next race. I'll put five shillings on it for you," Freddy said, half to spite his mother, half to please Eliza.

It was much more exciting when you had

money on a race. Eliza stood at the front of the box, with the champagne spinning in her head, and watched the horses all come round in a bunch into the straight.

"Come on, Dover!" At Ascot, nobody shouted at the horses, like they did at the Derby, but Dover was inching ahead, and he had Eliza's five bob on him.

"Come on," she yelled, waving her parasol. "Come on, you rotten mule. Run yer lousy guts out!"

It was over. " 'E got pipped at the post." She turned and saw all the snobby people in the box gaping at her, Higgins doubled up as if he was laughing — or dying, and the colonel reaching like a drowning man for a bottle of champagne.

Chapter 8

"WE HAVE TAUGHT HER how to speak," the professor said, talking across Eliza as if she were not there. "Now I think, my dear Pickering, we had better teach her to listen."

It was breakfast time on the day after the races. Eliza was sitting at her usual place halfway down the long mahogany table. Higgins and Pickering, like an allergic married couple, sat at opposite ends, so that Uncle Nutters and Mary Jane walked half a mile each meal to serve them.

"What's that you say?" The colonel cupped an ear with his hand.

"Sorry, mouthful of haddock."

The two men were eating their usual enormous breakfast of fish and eggs and sausages, and gallons of tea in giant cups like soup bowls, but Eliza could eat nothing. She sat humbly between them with her eyes cast down, a naughty child waiting to be punished.

Nothing much had been said yesterday. In the car on the way home, they slapped their knees and laughed, and spoke French to each other, which meant they were talking no good about Eliza. When they got home she said she had a headache, which was true, and went to bed before dinner.

When Mary Jane came up eager for news, she found the door bolted and Eliza pretending to be asleep.

This morning she would get it. This would be the end. Her last breakfast and she wouldn't eat a thing! What a waste.

"No thanks," she said to the scrambled egg and chicken livers. Mary Jane looked sorry for her, although she would gobble it herself in the serving pantry beyond the swing door.

What was the professor saying? He raised his voice and repeated down the length of white tablecloth, "I said, now we must teach her to listen."

"Teach?" Eliza raised her head.

"Every living creature, even a beetle or a haddock, knows how to listen. Only a chump like you has to be taught."

"Taught?"

"Don't keep repeating me like a machine.

What's the matter with you today, girl? You look like a sick cow."

"But I thought you weren't going to teach me any more." She looked down at the table-cloth, blurred through her tears.

"You thought you knew it all?"

"I thought you were throwing me out," she whispered, and the colonel called testily, "Eh? What — what's she say?"

"Throw you out — with the Embassy ball six weeks away and all London agog to meet you?"

"To laugh at me. I — I let you down. I shamed you in front of all them swells." She was talking broad cockney again. Might as well. She'd soon be back to it.

"No, you didn't, you stupid girl. They loved it."

"Didn't they guess then, that I was only a common flower girl?" She looked up at him with shining new hope, as if he were a god.

"Of course not. After the colonel whistled you off to the car, I explained about this cockney play you'd been rehearsing. In North-umberland. You were saying bits of your part. They thought it was terrific. Such a clever mimic. So much vitality." He imitated Mrs. Higgins' drawly voice. "My mother is wild to see you again. She's going to take you shop-ping, and to the art galleries, and to Gunter's for tea — oh, you're It, Eliza Doolittle!"

"Nah." The hope died into reality. He was just an ordinary man again, with a raw morning chin, and egg on his top lip. "I can't do it. That wasn't no play-acting. That was me."

"That was I."

"I . . . me . . . what's the difference? I *am* only a little cockney girl."

"You're not! You're Elizabeth Doolittle. *My* Elizabeth Doolittle." He reached out and took her hand.

"It's no good. I'll have to chuck it. I can't go to the ball."

"You can, and you will, and you'll be the loveliest woman there. You'll see. Oh, come on, Eliza, for my sake. I believe in you. Won't you believe in me?"

She nodded. He could charm the wallpaper off the wall, that man.

"What the deuce are you two whispering about?" The colonel threw down his napkin and got up. "If you're talking to me, I can't hear a word you're saying."

"We're saying we've got six weeks to do six years of work." Higgins got up. "Come on, everybody. Lessons."

Suddenly hungry, Eliza stayed behind to snatch a piece of toast. When she got to the door, she heard Higgins say exultantly, "We'll do it!"

Not, "She'll do it." Ho yus, charm the wallpaper all right, but he was still the sculptor Pygmalion, she still Galatea, his puppet: valuable only as an experiment, not for herself.

So naturally, when Freddy Eynsford-Hill came calling, loaded with violets and love, she encouraged him. He was allowed to visit her in the drawing room, where he sat adoring her with his eyes and laughing at everything she said, but Higgins would not let him take her for a walk, or for a drive in his new Lancia touring car.

"Why not?" Eliza protested. "He loves me for myself. I'm not a doll to him. I'm a real girl."

"Doll or girl, you're not going out alone with him," Higgins said. "He's too much of an ass to keep you out of trouble."

"Don't you speak like that about my feller," Eliza said sharply. "Are you jealous?"

"Oh, shut up," Higgins said. "Get on with the dictation."

As well as teaching her other important tasks, like how to toast his crumpets in front of the study fire, he had taught her to write letters, and part of her work now was to read and sort and answer the letters that came to him from all over the world. Mrs. Pearce and the maids were forbidden under threats of burning alive to touch his papers, or even to dust. But he had taught Eliza to take care of his desk and the file drawers and the tottering piles of work from his university students, which he was going to attend to some day.

One afternoon when Eliza was sorting papers, Mrs. Higgins came to the house in a swathed dress of Paisley silk with a ten-inch fringe round the hem.

"I didn't know she was your secretary, Henry."

"I just let her fool about. What do I need a secretary for?" He waved a hand at the chaos of books and notes and manuscripts on the desk. "Where the devil is the note I made about the musical sequence of the milkman's morning hymn of, 'Milko-o-o'?"

"You stuck it in a picture frame." Eliza pulled out a scribbled scrap of paper.

"She seems to be very useful to you," the professor's mother said. She had a jokey sort of voice, so that you were never sure if she were laughing or serious.

"She has her uses."

"But not today," his mother said. "Today we are going shopping."

"To Whiteleys?" Eliza loved to go shopping at Whiteleys.

"The Universal Provider?" Mrs. Higgins wrinkled her aristocratic nose, as if Whiteleys was bad drains. "They say, you know, that William Whiteley once boasted he could supply anything in the world. So a customer asked for a white elephant. And got it. No doubt an excellent store for elephants, Elizabeth, but for a ball gown, there's only *La Maison Française.*"

"Oh goodness, Mrs. Higgins, how glorious!" Four weeks ago, Eliza might still have said, "Oh crikey, how luverly." She still did, in the servants' hall, but the sight of anyone like Mrs. Higgins now automatically triggered off what the professor called her Elizabeth voice.

Eliza and Mrs. Higgins were becoming good friends. She was not nearly as alarming as Eliza had feared. She was not alarming at all, like Freddy's mother, or the hard and coldly elegant ladies they met when they were shopping, or having meringues and praline ices at fashionable Gunter's tearoom, or listening to military bands in Hyde Park, or any of the things that were right for a country girl from Northumberland to do. Although she had been born and bred among classy ladies like these, Mrs. Higgins laughed at their artificial airs. She was a rebel, like her son. You could see where he got it from.

If she had not promised to keep the secret, Eliza might have been tempted to tell Mrs. Higgins the truth. Perhaps she would, after the ball, when the bet was won and she was accepted everywhere by the lordliest in the land. It would be the sort of joke Mrs. Higgins would enjoy. But she was too loose-tongued to be trusted with the secret, so Eliza had to be careful to stick to the imaginary family history, in which Higgins and Pickering had drilled her dozens of times.

"Who are you?"

"Elizabeth Doolittle."

"Who is your father?"

"Sir Alfred Cornelius Doolittle, ex-President of the Southeast Malayan Rubber Company."

"Doolittle? That's a weird sort of name, my dear young lady."

This was the point of the lesson at which Eliza usually started to giggle. She had to pull down her mouth and think of something sad, before she could answer. "The name descends to us from our ancestors, Sir Charlebus DoLittle. So called because although he rode off to the Crusades, he was too gentlemanly to join in any of the killing."

"Why hasn't your mother taken you anywhere?"

A sigh. "She's not strong, poor Mother. All that time in the East, you know. Her blood is thin as water, the doctors say. We live very quietly in a small manor house in Northumberland. Only a hundred acres of land, but my father, like Sir Charlebus, does not believe in killing even a pheasant, so there are no shooting parties."

"Your mother comes originally from Norfolk, you say?" Mrs. Higgins asked, as they drove to the fashion salon of Madame Françoise in Mayfair. "And your father from Durham?"

"That's — I mean, yes."

"That's right" was one of the things you were not supposed to say, for some daft reason. It was ridiculous, the whole thing, but Eliza had worked at her new language so long and so hard that she could even detect a small mistake made by a society lady who was not as grand as she pretended.

"And yet, you know," mused Mrs. Higgins, "there is some charming quality in your speaking voice I can't quite place. A touch of French blood, perhaps?" (The professor had got his gifts for accents from her, as well as his rebelliousness.)

"That must be from my Great-aunt Clara," Eliza invented hastily. "In wines, her family was." Fairly pickled in wine, she had been, so it wasn't quite a lie, although the only French Aunt Clara knew was cognac.

"Whereabouts in France?"

Before Eliza could get tangled in her own inventions, they arrived at the salon, and the next two hours were a dream of satins and laces and chiffons and pearls, and French women (relations of Aunt Clara?) crying, "But, mademoiselle, ees bee-oo-tee-fool!"

Higgins and Pickering were not allowed to see the gown until the evening of the ball.

When Eliza came down to the drawing room, where they were formally awaiting her, she found all the servants lined up before the door in a guard of honor. The cook, the kitchenmaid, the housemaid, Mary Jane, Mrs. Pearce, Uncle Nutters — they all embraced her and wished her luck. It was a moment of great emotion. Eliza felt that all her life had been leading toward this one evening.

"If that Freddy don't pop the question tonight," Mary Jane whispered as she kissed her, "he's a bigger fool than he looks."

But that was not the excitement that gripped Eliza's heart so that she could hardly speak. It was something much more important. It was the proving of herself. Perhaps tonight she would find out who she really was.

Who am I?

As if in answer, Uncle Nutters flung open the door, flung out his narrow chest, and flung his grandest master-of-ceremonies voice into the drawing room.

"Miss Elizabeth Doolittle!"

Eliza stepped forward into the middle of the room and stood, knowing what she looked like, waiting to be told that she was beautiful.

Higgins and Pickering were standing by the white marble fireplace, splendid in their swallowtail coats and white waistcoats, a whole kaleidoscope of medals decorating one side of the colonel's chest. For a moment, they did not move or speak. "Struck dumb by me beauty." The phrase popped into Eliza's head, and her mouth twitched, but she would not let it giggle. Then the colonel's monocle fell out and he lunged forward like a hippopotamus who has seen its mate.

"Eliza," he said, very moved. "Oh, my dear girl, you are the most divine vision that ever delighted these wicked old eyes."

"Thank you, Colonel Pick." She tapped

him lightly with her fan, as girls like Tennyson's Maud did when they were flirting.

"What do you say, Higgins, what do you say? Would you believe she —"

The professor was pacing toward her, his head down and his hands behind his back. He circled her once, twice, eyes narrowed, inspecting it all: the floating white and silver dress, all sewn with pearls and diamanté flowers, the tiara in the shining coiled hair and the diamonds round her white throat, that were no less dazzling for being hired for the night.

"London Bridge is falling down . . ." Softly he started to sing the old rhyme he had so often forced her to say through a mouthful of marbles.

> . . . falling down, falling down.
> London Bridge is falling down,
> My fair lady!

It was the nicest compliment he had ever paid her.

"But I can't do it, you know." Eliza stood before them, trembling. "They'll see through me, like they should have done at the races. I can't do it."

The Embassy ball had hung before her like a glittering treasure, beckoning her on. Now suddenly she wanted to turn and run and hide and be a nobody.

"You *can* do it." Higgins put his hand on

her arm to stop her shaking, "You can do anything."

Outside in the hall, a clamor of loud mouth and loud boots. Nutterville opened the door and said, of all things, "Miss Eliza's father is here."

"Oh, *no!*"

Oh, no, not now. Why did he have to come now? But Higgins said, "Bring him in, bring him in. A bit of comic relief. Just what we need. Welcome, my dear Doolittle." For Eliza's father was already pushing in past Nutterville, not being a man to be kept standing in hallways. "And whom have I the honor — ?"

For Alfred Doolittle was not alone. A few paces behind, in a purple bonnet and cape, jaw clenched like a fist to show she was not impressed by the address, was his landlady, Mrs. Hardcastle.

"This here is the lady I told you about. Mrs. Prunella — Blimey." He took a second look at the vision in the middle of the room. "Eliza!"

"If you've come here for money," she said in her carefully cultured voice, "you're wasting your time."

"That's a nice thing for a father to hear from the lips of 'is only child." He appealed to the room. "It don't look like me daughter. It don't sound like me daughter. But s'welp me, it's the sort of thing me daughter would say."

"I know you," Eliza said, aware that she was saying the old kind of things to him, but in a new kind of voice. "You're up to something."

"It so happens," her father said with dignity, "that the only thing I'm up to is matrimony." He drew Mrs. Hardcastle forward, the hatpins in her purple bonnet bristling like a porcupine. "Your new stepmother. Professor 'Iggins. Colonel What's-'is-name. My fiongsay."

"Your what?" Eliza's jaw hung.

"I come here to tell you that Mrs. H. is going to do me the honor of becoming Mrs. D. Nothing for it," he whispered hoarsely to Eliza, under the cover of general commotion of congratulations and the pouring of wine to celebrate. "Four months behind on me rent, she's got me trapped. Though if you could slip me five quid, I might still —"

"The bride and groom!" Higgins raised his glass.

Mrs. Hardcastle drank with little sipping pecks, like a finicky hen. Mr. Doolittle tipped back his glass and smacked his lips gloomily.

"Why's that girl dressed up like her own funeral?" he wanted to know.

"I'm going to a ball, Father."

"Ai'm going to a bawl, Fahthah." He mimicked her voice. "What do you think of that, Prunella?"

"I wouldn't know her," Mrs. Hardcastle

said, then added sharply, in case that might be taken as flattery, "That dress is cut very low."

"Father from Leeds, mother Welsh — no, Cheshire," Higgins murmured automatically, and Prunella said, "I beg *yours!*" and raked him up and down with her military eye.

"I'm forced to say," Alfred Doolittle was walking round Eliza as if she were a horse at auction, "you've done a good job, professor. Cinderella at the ball, eh?"

"Tonight Eliza makes her entry into society at the Transylvanian Embassy."

"You'll never get away with it." Doolittle shook his head with the wisdom of a man who has tried to get away with many things, and failed. "They'll rumble 'er, you'll see. Dresses, jools, sparklers in 'er hair — she's still a plain street girl, when all's said and done. Just because you've taught 'er to speak all la-di-da don't make no difference."

"But it does! Her speech makes her a different person, don't you see? That's what I'm trying to prove. It's the bridge across the huge gulf that separates class from class, soul from soul."

"I got a nice one of them," Alfred Doolittle said. "That balmy old millionaire in America, what yer wrote to, he likes my soul so much, he wants me to go over there and give a talk about right and wrong."

"Why don't you?" Eliza asked. Anything would be better than marrying his landlady.

"*She* wouldn't let me." He jerked his head

at Mrs. Hardcastle, who did not like the wine or the turn of the conversation, and was on her way out. "She'd have the seaports watched, have me arrested at the gangway. Well, ta-ta for now, girl. After tonight, I may see yer back in the market. Bring me one of them di-mins bright, if yer can get away with it." He blew Eliza a kiss, waved a hand at the professor, and saluted the colonel.

" 'Ow do?" he said genially to Mrs. Higgins, meeting her in the hall in old-rose brocade, ablaze with family jewels.

"How do?" she said, unsurprised. You never knew who you would meet at Henry's. "What market?" she asked, gliding into the drawing room, but was too entranced with the sight of Eliza to notice that nobody answered.

In the car she told them casually, "I understand the Queen of Transylvania is here on a visit, and will be at the ball."

A queen! Eliza went white and almost jumped out of the car, but Higgins rubbed his hands and asked, "Just what we need."

"And you'll be able to meet that marvelous Hungarian everyone talks about. The great speech expert, Professor Karpathy. He goes everywhere with the queen, to protect her, because he can spot an imposter, they say, as soon as he opens his mouth. He knows almost as much about languages as you do, dear. You'll have *so* much in common."

"Won't we?" Higgins looked a little sick,

and the colonel groaned under his breath. "Just our blithering luck."

"Let's go home." Eliza panicked, and Mrs. Higgins glanced at her quickly.

"Nonsense, child. Have you never met royalty before?"

The Transylvanian Embassy was a vast white house in Belgrave Square, with a blaze of lights and flowers and polished floors, and a great many handsome menservants whom Eliza thought were guests, until Higgins poked her in the ribs for smiling at them. The great ballroom was at the bottom of a wide curving staircase. You had to walk down it alone, while the handsomest manservant of all, in a scarlet jacket and white knee breeches, roared your name to wake the dead.

"Lord and Lady Mountfitchet!"

"Sir Reginald and Lady Tarrington!"

"His Excellency Count Oswald Ziludski!"

"I can't —" Eliza shrank back, and met the stern waistcoat of Higgins, cutting off retreat.

"Get down there," he snarled out of the side of his mouth, "or I'll send you back to your stepmother."

She walked forward, gave her name.

"Miss Elizabeth Doolittle!"

The ballroom held its breath. It seemed that all the faces looked up, like flowers turning to the sun. It seemed that all the crystal drops in the great chandeliers shed sparkling tears of gladness. It seemed that the band struck up a triumphal march just for her, as she paced down the stairs and touched finger-tips with the ambassador and his wife, and curtsied low to the Queen of Transylvania, a smiling plump old lady who looked — so this was royalty! — like Mrs. Pearce.

Freddy was there, of course. He had got himself an invitation when he found out Eliza was going. His mother was in full sail as usual, billowing across the floor in waltz time in a lavender organdy rig about thirty years too young for her. Freddy was waiting behind a pillar to spring out at Eliza and stammer, "I say, Miss Doo, you look smashing. You must give me all the dances on your p-p-p-ro-gramme."

"Now, now, my boy, don't be selfish." Higgins took Eliza round the waist himself. "To get your sea legs," he murmured in her ear, keeping her in the middle of the crowded floor until he saw how she went.

"How did she go?" the colonel whispered anxiously when they joined him in a bower of potted palms under the balcony. You'd think she was a car.

"Like a bird," said Higgins. "Those dancing lessons are worth every penny you're going to pay for them."

"If I pay." He looked gloomy. "I've just seen that villain Karpathy."

"How does he look?"

"Like a black bear. And he was staring at Eliza as if she were a pot of honey."

"I'll go and scout out the lie of the land.

Here you are, young man." As Freddy came hopefully up, the professor passed over Eliza's hand with a flourish. "She's all yours."

"I wish you were," Freddy said, as he danced her away. "Golly, Miss Doo, you turkey trot like an angel."

"I've asked you a thousand times to call me Elizabeth," she said loftily. She was not afraid anymore. She was Cinderella in her glory, on wings in fairyland. But she kept glimpsing princes much more charming than the chinless one who held her as cautiously as fragile china. It seemed a waste to be in a glittering dress at a glittering ball and have only Freddy, whom she could have any day, perched on the sofa guffawing at her jokes.

When the music stopped he took her out to walk on the terrace. It was a perfect night. Beyond the lighted terrace, the dark trees and bushes of the Embassy garden bloomed with tiny colored lanterns. Romantic. And all she had was Freddy, asking, "Say some of that funny slang for me, Miss — er Lizbeth."

"I can't," she said. "It's not allowed. Don't bother me."

She turned away from him, but he picked up her gloved hand from the balustrade. "Be nice to me," he pleaded, and she was reminded with a jolt of poor Billy with his thatch of yellow hair and his empty blue eyes. Why did she always get the soppy, doglike ones?

"I s-s-say." Freddy struggled wetly to give

voice to his feelings. "Wouldn't it be s-s-simply ripping if you and I got hitched?"

"No," she said unkindly. Some proposal! "It wouldn't."

"I'll sit on your doorstep. You'll fall over me every time you come out."

"I'll go out the back."

"I'll sit there till you say yes."

"You're going to have an awfully cold winter," she said briskly. "Don't be such a bore, Freddy. Let's dance. That's something you do quite well, at least."

"Golly — thanks." You could not even insult him.

When they came round to the opposite corner, Higgins went, "Psst! psst!" like a spy, and beckoned her from under the balcony.

"Your mother wants you." She pushed Freddy in the opposite direction, and joined Higgins and Pickering among the potted palms.

"You're doing splendidly," Higgins reported. "The ambassador and his wife say they are enchanted with you, and so does the queen, if she could speak English. Now they've got this blasted bearded Hungarian interested, and he wants to meet you."

She nodded, eyes sparkling, silver slipper tapping to the music. People glanced at her admiringly as they danced by. She felt equal to anything.

"Avoid him," the Professor said dramatically, "at all costs. He's out to sink us. I've had a chat with him. He's brilliant, but he's crooked. He teaches people new voices to disguise their real identity —"

"Like you with me." She giggled.

"— and then demands money not to give them away."

"Blackmail," the colonel said darkly. "That dirty bearded Balkan."

But the dirty bearded Balkan was cleverer than they were. Between themselves and Freddy, they kept her away from him until just before supper. Then a footman came to Higgins. "Telephone call for you, Professor. Urgent." And almost immediately, a page boy came to tell the colonel the same thing.

"Let's get some grub, old girl," Freddy said in his romantic way, but a great grizzly of a man with a wide black beard that reached to the middle of his shirt front was bowing before Eliza.

"Allow me to present myself, my dear Miss Doolittle. Professor Zoltan Karpathy, from Budapest, your partner for supper."

Eliza looked round in a fluster, but there was only moonfaced Freddy, letting her go to her doom without lifting a finger. Offering her his arm, Karpathy steered her toward the buffet. To pull away or make a fuss would be worse than to go with him. She held up her head and tried to look as if he were her choice for supper, as he nodded and smiled and greeted people and introduced her: "The faymuzz Meez Doo-liddle."

"Why am I famous?" she asked when they reached the long buffet, which had enough meats and poultry and hams and towering cakes and jellies on it to feed all the Covent Garden porters for a year.

"Because you are beautiful, and alzo mysterious. Everyone vant to know: 'Who is she?' I alone shall discover."

"You know who I am," she said. "I'm Elizabeth Doolittle."

"Aha." He put a finger to his nose and winked at her, like a sinister goblin. "Now led us zee . . . pheasant in aspeec . . . saddle of venison . . . lobster zalad . . ." He filled her plate with exquisite food, and brought her champagne.

"If you're such a great language expert," she said, when they were sitting on a little brocaded settee in an alcove, "why do you talk with such a thick accent?"

"If I didn't," he said in perfect English, "nobody would believe I was Hungarian. You should know that." He bent forward and put her under the microscope of his bright little black eyes.

There was a catch in that remark somewhere. Watch out, Eliza.

Nervous as she was, she could not help eating. This was the first time she had ever seen such sumptuous food – and probably the last, if the game was up.

He questioned her for what seemed like hours, listening carefully to her careful voice, his black button eyes observing the way she held her fork, the way she drank. Out of the corner of her eye, she saw Higgins and Pickering in the doorway. When they saw her, they slumped, and went dejectedly out onto the terrace, without even looking at the display of food on the buffet.

"That is a very pretty fairy tale," Zoltan Karpathy said finally, when she told him all her practiced story, plus a lot she had heroically invented. "You're a good liar. Now I want the truth."

So it was all up. Born Lisson Grove. Poorhouse School. Shirt factory. Street seller. She might as well tell him the whole of it before he guessed at something even worse.

"May I have some more champagne?" she asked desperately. She would run while he was gone for it.

"At your command." He plucked a glass off the tray of a passing waiter. "Your health, princess." He raised his glass.

"Don't make fun of me." Eliza looked down at her pearl and silver lap.

"Fun — no. Impertinence — yes, perhaps, your highness. You have your own reasons for remaining incognito. I shall honor your secret. I just want you to know that the great Karpathy is not deceived. Your English is perfect. Too perfect. These idle Anglo-Saxons never bother to learn their own language properly. Your vowel sounds reveal to me most clearly that you are Hungarian. I knew it half an hour ago, but it was when you said 'champagne' with that slight, that exquisite, hint of 'cham-*pyne*' that your royal blood was revealed." He stood up. "Au revoir, princess." He bowed low, and tickled the back of her hand with his whiskers. "Enjoy yourself. My lips are sealed."

He walked away with his finger to the hole in his beard where his mouth was. A duchess claimed him, and he started to talk his gargling broken English again.

Elizabeth sat in the alcove paralyzed. Then a slow serene smile spread over her face, and she rose, and walked very regally out to the terrace, to give her subjects the royal proclamation: "I did it!"

The terrace was empty. She found them halfway down the garden, sitting miserably on the plinth of a statue of Venus with their backs against the legs of the goddess.

When they saw her dress shimmering before them in the shadows, they raised their eyes but not their heads, like beaten men.

"I did it," she said quietly, and told them what had happened.

"We did it!" They both jumped up, grabbed her hands, and romped round the statue like drunken revelers in Picadilly Circus.

"I win the bet! I win, I win!" Higgins shouted to the night, and a young man and a girl came round from behind a laurel bush to look at him.

"We did it," he told them, "and he'll have to pay all the bills."

"I don't care." The colonel wagged his bald head. "We did it!"

Arm in arm, they reeled back indoors for champagne. Eliza followed. She was always following Higgins, who was never gentlemanly enough to let her go ahead, unless it was somewhere he didn't want to go, like down the Embassy stairs into the ballroom.

The Queen of Transylvania and Professor Karpathy had left. Now that she was free to talk to anyone, Eliza was the queen. Good Queen Bess — Oh, Mum, if you were here to see me now! Everyone wanted to meet her, to admire her, to dance with her. She flung herself so furiously into the party that she did not see Higgins until it was over.

"The belle of the ball!" Mrs. Higgins put her cloak round her with a friendly embrace, then took a closer look. "What's the matter, child?"

"Nothing." How could Eliza stamp her foot and say, "*He* didn't do it — I did!"

But Mrs. Higgins was nobody's fool. "Henry?" she asked.

Eliza nodded, and immediately would have given anything to have the nod back. Now it would be all round London that she was in love with the man she hated most in all the world.

Chapter 9

At home, all the servants who were as excited about Eliza as if she were their champion racehorse, had waited up to hear if she had won.

"We did it!" Higgins cried out as he came into the house, and they came sleepily out onto the staircase, beaming down on him like frowsy cherubs.

"I did it!" he proclaimed, swaggering on the black and white tiles of the hall, with his top hat and his silk-lined cloak and his ebony cane. "She was the sensation of the evening. I fooled them all. I proved it can be done."

Everyone crowded into the study, and there was a great celebration, with congratulations and rejoicing and the colonel dancing a jig, and the kitchenmaid, who was only fifteen, curled up in the colonel's deep armchair with her shoes off, snoring.

Everyone kissed "the princess" and Mrs. Pearce was so carried away by emotion that she actually kissed the professor, and said huskily, "God bless you, sir."

"I am the great Pygmalion," the professor chanted. "Behold, my living statue, my Galatea. Though I must give credit," he admitted, happily generous, "where credit is due."

Ah well, Eliza thought, at last he's getting round to it, and none too soon.

"Let's not forget," he reminded Nutters and Mrs. Pearce and Mary Jane and the cook and the housemaid and the sleeping kitchenmaid, "let us not forget the one who has worked with me day in, day out, cheerful, helpful, the truest of companions through thick and thin —"

Blimey, 'Enry 'Iggins, Eliza thought, in cockney, don't swell me 'ead.

"— my excellent friend, Colonel James Arbuthnot Pickering! We did it, Pickering!"

"We did it, Higgins!"

"A victory song!" the professor cried. "Eliza's song!" The colonel began to thump on the piano and everyone joined in:

My old man said, "Foller the van,
And don't dillydally on the wye."
Off went the van wiv me 'ome packed in it . . .

Eliza slipped away while they were singing.

. . . can't trust a special like an old time copper,
When you can't find your wye 'ome!

The raucous music followed her as she
stumbled down the stairs in her tight skirt,
and went along the basement passage to the
butler's pantry.

It was dark. Joey was asleep, but he took
his head out from under his wing to chirp at
her. She opened the cage, and took him out on
her finger.

"Pretty Liza, pretty Liza." He pecked at
the diamond earrings, due to go back to the
shop for it was already tomorrow. "Joey,
Joey, Joey."

He was the same anyway. Everything else
was spoiled and rotten, but birds and animals never let you down.

"Eliza?" The opening door threw in a shaft
of flickering gaslight from the passage. "What
are you doing down here in the dark?"

"Talking to my Joe." The bird nibbled at
her hair.

"I saw you sneak away." Uncle Nutters put
his arm round her weary shoulders. "What's
up, mate?"

"I hate him." She turned round. She was
taller than the butler even without her party
heels. "I hate them both, conceited, selfish

beasts. 'We did it, Higgins. We did it, Pickering.' Who did it? That's what I want to know. *Who* did it?"

"Why you, of course." Nutterville struck a match and reached up on tiptoe to light the gas. In this kind of house, the folk upstairs had electric light. The folk downstairs still had gas.

"That's just it." She looked down at his worried monkey face, creased with pity for her, and saw that he was the only one who cared. "They don't care about me," she said bitterly. "I've won their stupid bet for them. I've been through the tortures of hell these last six months, you know I have. I went through worse tonight, with that bearded spy. And what thanks do I get? Oh, Uncle Nutters, it's all so beastly, whatever shall I do?"

"Why don't you chuck it?" he said. "You've had a taste of this life, and those kind of people." He jerked his chin upward. "Why don't you go back to your own folk?"

"My dad? That woman?" She could not get her lips round the word stepmother, if it applied to Mrs. Hardcastle. "You can't go back. I found that out ages ago."

"He'll drop you though." Nutters was not disloyal to his boss, but honest. "He's finished with you, you'll see. You won his bet for him, that's all he wanted from you. When I was a jockey, I remember there was a horse won six big races in a row. The stable's darling, he was. Pint of beer every day. Pure wool blanket. Best wheat straw. The lot. Then he went lame, and couldn't race again. The owner sold him to a dealer and he ended up drawing a junk cart, with his hipbones and ribs sticking out like the old iron he was pulling. Dropped that horse, he did, when it was no more use to him. Just like the professor will drop you."

"I can't believe that," Eliza said. "He can't be as heartless as that."

"Ten minutes ago, you thought he could. 'He doesn't care,' you said. I've known him longer than you, me old mate, and I'm afraid you might be right."

But Uncle Nutters was disillusioned by a hard life, first as a stable boy up at five to knock ice out of buckets, then as a jockey, drinking vinegar to lose weight, then as a butler, serving with food and drink the kind of people who had once served him cheers and praise when he won money for them on the racecourse.

Life could not be as unfair as all that. The next morning, Eliza woke more cheerful, and knew that everything would be all right. There were telephone calls, invitations, flowers arriving for her. She was a smash hit in society, and this morning Higgins would see her with fresh eyes, as a somebody in her own right.

The only trouble was, he was not there to

see her. He had breakfasted very early, and was shut in the study with a notice on the door saying, "Everyone but ME — Keep Out!"

Eliza was hovering uncertainly outside, wondering whether she should knock, or wait till lunchtime, when she heard Freddy come into the hall, asking for her.

She moved back, so that he would not see her at the top of the staircase, and when Nutterville came up with more roses, she said, "Tell him I'm out, or ill, or broken my leg. Get rid of him."

"He won't be got rid of. He's been sitting on that doorstep since nine o'clock this morning. Only gets up to go and buy more flowers, and then he sits down again. Anyone who comes to the door has to step over him. It's quite inconvenient."

"Tell him —"

From behind the study door came a shout: "Eliza! Where the deuce — Eliza!" and she went in without a backward glance.

Higgins was crouched over the desk, with a jumble of papers and notebooks all round him, books and crumpled balls of paper on the floor, the wastebasket frothing over like beer, the drawers she kept so tidy half open, and spilling out old letters and torn magazine cuttings and loops of typewriter ribbon.

"Where's the story I cut out of the *Times*, about the deaf and dumb Mongolian?" he grunted, without looking up at her.

She went to the right file, found it at once, and gave it to him. He took it without thanks, and then, aware that she was still standing behind him, said irritably, "Run away, I'm working."

"I just —" She had rehearsed something to say to get his attention if she got the chance.

"Later."

"I just wanted to ask you. Remember that wallpaper we saw with all the little rosebuds and the chintz material to match, and you said we might redecorate my room?"

He grunted, writing.

"Well, I thought, as everything went so well last night, perhaps I could —"

"Not now, not now. Why do you bother me with such rubbish now?"

"Are you busy?" she asked stupidly.

"Busy! I'm writing the chronicle of my great experiment. I'm constructing the classic document that will be read with awe and wonder all over the world, and she asks me, 'Are you busy?' "

"I only thought —"

"Don't you realize, girl?" He threw down his pen and leaned back, running a hand through his soft untidy hair. "This is the most important thing in my whole life. What I've done will make language history."

"What *you've* done! Oh, cripes!"

"Cripes, Eliza?" he repeated mildly. "Do I allow that word?"

"It's the only one to express how I feel." She stood across the desk from him, hands on hips, feeling her face burn red and her skin prickle with rage.

"If you're angry because of the wallpaper," he said blindly, "go out and order it. We've spent so much on you already, a bit more won't matter."

"I didn't ask you to spend nothing. Anything. Take it all back. I don't want it."

He raised an eyebrow calmly. "The diamonds have got to be sent back today anyway, since they were rented."

"And so was I! You gave my dad five pounds for me, and don't deny it. Rented for your experiment, that's all I was, and now I'm no more use to you than that poor lame racehorse."

"What horse? What on earth are you talking about?"

"What happens to me now? Am I to be sent back, like the diamonds?"

"You're free to do what you want, of course. You always have been."

"That's a lie, for a start." Eliza laughed without mirth. "And what am I fit to do? I can't go back. I can't stay here. I don't belong anywhere, thanks to you."

"I said you could stay here, if that's what you want." Higgins took off the thick-rimmed glasses he wore for work, and rubbed his eyes wearily.

"I wouldn't stay here if you was the King of England," Eliza said with great scorn.

"If I were the King, the Queen wouldn't let you." He put on his glasses, picked up his pen, and bent over his papers again.

"Because I'm pretty? Look at me!" She snatched up a notebook and threw it at his head. "You think I'm pretty?"

"Not bad." He rubbed his head, but did not look up. "I don't see why you're so fussed about your future. You can get Freddy, or some other well-born chinless wonder, to marry you, I'm sure."

"I'd rather be dead."

"Or we could set you up in that flower shop you used to keep talking about."

"Ooh — you devil! Buy me off, is that the idea?" She lunged round the desk and hit him, and he was angry now at last. Cursing, he jumped up and dodged round to keep the desk between them.

"Wait till I get you — Pygmalion!" She laughed wildly, her hands grabbing the air like claws. "Pig, more like. Pig, pig, pig!"

"I was wrong," he said, trying to recover his temper, but still flushed and breathing fast. "I'm Frankenstein, not Pygmalion. It's not Galatea I've made, but a little spitting monster."

"*You* made! *You* made! Oh —" She beat childishly on the desk with her fists. "You're the most hateful, conceited man I ever met!"

She ran out of the room in tears, down the staircase, and out of the front door, banging it with a thunderous crash that she hoped would bring the house down.

Freddy was still sitting on the doorstep. "Come on." She called him like a pet dog, and marched off up the street. He caught her up as she crossed the main road and turned into Regent's Park.

"What's the matter, Lizbeth?" he asked panting and blinking. "Has something upset you?"

"Upset me!" She flung herself down on the cool sweet grass among the children and nursemaids and doll prams and hoops and pet poodles. "I'm so angry, I could kill myself."

"You don't have to do that," he said hopefully. "You can marry me."

"What on? I'm not going to live off your mother. You'd have to get a job."

"A job?" He had put down a newspaper to sit on, careful of his elegant pale trousers. "What do you mean, a job?" She might have said the moon.

"We could live cheaply enough, two rooms somewhere, and I could get a job in a flower shop. Get my own business, after a bit, if we —"

"But, my dear." Freddy was beginning to look very shocked. "You don't know what you're saying. Two rooms — you're joking.

How could we entertain? And then there's the Season, Ascot, the Riviera. . . . It will have to be a very successful flower shop."

"Where I come from," Eliza got up, "women don't work to support useless men."

Though that's just what my poor mum did, she thought, running away across the grass.

"Where are you going?" Freddy was gasping behind.

"Back where I come from!" A taxi was standing outside the Park gates. She jumped into it and slammed the door in poor Freddy's face, open-mouthed to ask, "Where?"

In Covent Garden, the early morning rush of buying and selling was over. The vans of the wholesalers and the big shops had gone. Only a few pony carts and some of the barrows that went out later to sell off the small stuff were standing about among the arches and worn stone pillars. The ponies wore nosebags and were blowing chaff among the trodden cabbage leaves on the cobbles. The porters and costermongers were lunching too, lounging round the stall that sold hot pies and blood sausage, with tin mugs of tea and the cigar ends they picked up outside the Opera House.

As Eliza approached, picking her way carefully over the piles of vegetable rubbish, they looked at her without curiosity, for ladies and gents quite often took the short cut

through the market from the Strand to Long-
acre, or came poking about, absorbing the
atmosphere of colorful Old London.

"You looking for something, lady?" a man
in a checked cap asked, as she hesitated a
few yards from the pie stall.

"Yes. Do you know someone called —" The
group of people shifted a little, and she saw
that one of them was Billy. He had his arm
around a stout girl with a greasy red face
and hair that had not been washed for weeks.

"Called what?" The man was Eliza's old
chum Charlie Price. He did not recognize her
with her hair piled up high and her pink and
white linen dress, and of course her new voice.

Billy did not recognize her either. She
smiled at him, but he looked through her
with that vacant blue stare. She could have
spoken to him in her old voice, but that girl
—"Oh, someone I used to know," she said
vaguely. "I don't think he's here any more."

"Blimey, I don't think anyone you'd know
would be lunchin' 'ere, miss," Charlie Price
said, and they all tittered. Billy pinched the
greasy-faced girl and she squealed like a pig.

"But thank you very much all the same,"
Eliza said, and as she turned away, the girl
tried a bad imitation, "Thenk yew veddy
much," and squawked with mocking laughter.

The house in Euston Road looked so different that Eliza walked past it, then came back

when she saw the number on the grimy fan-light over the next front door. Mrs. Hard-castle's house had come into money. The doors and window frames and the new window boxes stuck with artificial flowers were painted a curious shade of glistening violet. All the windows had new frilly white curtains, looping, and swooping and tied with great satin bows. The iron railings above the basement steps were gilded, with silver tips. The little tarnished frame that used to hold cards with names of lodgers, some long gone, had been replaced by a dazzling brass plaque that said, "Mr. and Mrs. Alfred Doolittle. Knock and Ring."

Eliza did both. It was necessary, to be heard over the noise of a Gramophone in the front room, and a lot of chatter and clatter from the kitchen at the back. A small hungry girl with a sore face and a rumpled apron opened the door, and Eliza followed the noise into the front room, getting a glimpse down the passage of several overweight people stuffing their mouths round a loaded table in the kitchen, where it had once been like a treasure hunt to find a crust of bread.

The front parlor, always empty before, and sheeted, as if the furniture were dead, now contained Mr. and Mrs. Alfred Doolittle on uncomfortable brocade chairs, wearing their best clothes and listening to a Gramophone blaring out ragtime music through its wide green horn.

"Good afternoon, miss," sniffed Mrs. Hardcastle. Eliza would cut out her tongue before she would address her, or even think of her as Mrs. Doolittle.

" 'Ow do," her father said unhappily turning his whole body to look at her, since his neck was clamped in a collar made for a giraffe.

It was not Mrs. Hardcastle or her house that had come into money. It was Alfred Doolittle. "Remember that American millionaire?" he said mournfully. "You know what he done? He up and died and left me four thousand pounds."

"Four thousand pounds! You could live in a palace."

He slid his eyes round to his wife, who was wearing plumcolored satin with a monkey fur collar and fur round the hem, although it was warm outside and baking in the parlor, whose windows were nailed up because of burglars. "She wants to stay here, so we can impress the neighbors."

"It's — it's wonderful for you, Dad."

The record ground to a stop and Prunella wound up the machine grimly and put on a tinny tango.

"Not really. I was better off before," Doolittle said under cover of the noise. "Now I'm respectable, it ain't half so much fun. That's what your precious 'Iggins has done by messing about with millionaires."

"Not my Higgins any more."

"Kicked you out, eh? I said he would. Well, if he thinks I'm going to keep you, you just go right back and prove him wrong, because I ain't. Got troubles enough of me own." He leaned closer and whispered, although the tango was so loud you could not have heard an elephant trumpet. "She's spending my money like water. Got all her relations in the kitchen there, swilling and guzzling. And the worst of it is, girl, if I'd only known old Wallingford was going to kick the bucket and leave me all this lolly, I never need have married her!"

Chapter 10

ELIZA HAD SOME MONEY in her pocket when she stormed out of 27a Wimpole Street that morning. She bought a carpetbag and filled it with newspapers, so that the maid in the dingy little hotel by the railway station should think it was proper luggage.

She spent all the evening reading the Situations Vacant advertisements in the newspapers, and all the next two days in employment agencies, looking for a job. At last she was offered an interview with a couple seeking a governess for three children in a country house in, of all places, Northumberland, home county of that belle of the ball, Miss Elizabeth Doolittle.

Her pink linen dress was now too crumpled

and dirty to wear for an interview, so she had to go back to Wimpole Street to get something to wear. She would leave all her fine clothes behind, and Higgins could sell them, or give them to the next girl who was unlucky enough to be one of his experiments. She would take only the plain skirts and blouses she used to wear when she was struggling over the Rine in Spine, and Come Inter the Garding, Mawd.

She went in at the kitchen entrance, and at once the hullabaloo started. Where had she been? What had happened? Had she been kidnapped? Why had she run away without telling anyone?

"What did you expect me to do?" she asked. "Send you a telegram: 'Safe and well, wish you were here?' "

"I wasn't worried," Uncle Nutters said, although she noticed that the nails of his well-kept butler's hands were bitten down flat. "Mrs. Pearce said we'd seen the last of you, but I knew you'd come back."

"I've only come for something to wear."

"What about the bird?" he said. "I knew you'd come back because of the bird."

"Yes. Joey." She saw herself stepping off the train at some tiny backwater station in Northumberland where the signalman grew prize geraniums to pass the time between trains, with her carpetbag in one hand and her birdcage in the other.

"Where on earth have you been, Elizabeth?" Mrs. Higgins came down to the kitchen, since everybody was too busy exclaiming over Eliza to answer the bell she had been ringing. "We've had the police out searching, detectives, bloodhounds — you never saw such a hue and a cry."

"I went back." Mrs. Higgins would think she meant back to Sir Alfred and Lady Doolittle in Northumberland.

But Mrs. Higgins did not think that. "To Covent Garden?" she asked quite casually.

"He told you." The rat. It didn't matter about anyone else, but for some reason, it was important that Mrs. Higgins should still believe in her.

"No." The professor's mother smiled. "I knew Henry was up to some game, of course, before he ever let me meet you. I'm not as simple as he thinks. But when I saw you, I recognized you immediately. You once sold me flowers, three years ago, when my husband was still alive. He bought me a buttonhole, and he gave you a shilling extra because you looked cold and hungry. 'Good luck, sir,' you said, but you had better luck than he did. He lost his life soon after. You found yours."

"Why did you never tell?" Eliza asked. "Why did you let me make a fool of myself, thinking you believed in me?"

"You were never a fool, my dear. And I

have believed in you all along. I didn't want to spoil it. I wanted us to be proper friends. We are still friends, aren't we?"

"Yes." The older woman's smile was so warm and coaxing that Eliza had to smile too. "But I'm never coming back," she added fiercely.

"Pity. My spoiled son has been quite lost without you," Mrs. Higgins said in the voice that might or might not be a joke. "It's the first thing he's wanted that he couldn't have."

"He don't want me. He doesn't —"

"Mother!" Higgins was yelling down the back stairs. "What on earth are you doing? Are you bringing the soda water?"

His mother grinned, and nodded to Eliza. She went to the bottom of the stairs, which ran up with an angled turn, so that she was hidden.

"Comin' up right awye," she called, in the old voice.

"Eliza," he said severely, "where the devil have you been?"

"None of your business."

"Isn't that just like a woman? Here's everybody been worried sick, half the police in London out looking for you, ships at Tilbury Docks searched, the Regent's Canal dragged for your body, and you say, 'None of your business.' Well, it's my own fault. I wanted to change you from a street urchin into a real, complicated woman. At least I've done that."

"I thought you didn't like women!" They were shouting up and down the stairs, still out of sight of each other, with Mrs. Higgins and all the servants enjoying it like a Punch and Judy show.

"I don't, when they're like you!"

"How did you ever learn manners, with Henry around?" Mrs. Higgins asked pleasantly.

"Colonel Pickering taught me all that side of it," Eliza answered, loud enough for Higgins to hear.

"I've taught her everything she knows," he shouted back. "I've wasted months of effort and a lifetime of precious knowledge on this — this ungrateful squashed cabbage leaf — this heartless market guttersnipe!"

"You watch your tongue, 'Iggins, there's ladies present. Very respectable too, I am. Going to be a governess."

"What will you teach?" He was taken aback.

"Oh — I dunno. Phonetics probably. Tennyson. I may even get to the end of that poem before I get the sack. Find out if Maud ever got into that blasted garden."

"You'll never get away with it on your own."

"The world hasn't stopped, you know, because I've left you. I'll get along all right."

Mrs. Higgins nodded and made applauding gestures, and Mary Jane, hiding in the broom cupboard, shouted faintly, "Hooray!"

She shut the cupboard door quickly as Higgins came down to the turn of the stairs to say sulkily, "I suppose you've never thought how I'll get along without you."

"You got along before I came," Eliza retorted, hiding her surprise.

"Who'll write my letters? Who will keep my engagements straight? I missed my appointment with the dentist yesterday. Who'll toast my crumpets just the way I like? Dash it, Eliza, I've got used to having you here."

"Too bad." She pushed past him, and went with dignity up the stairs.

The door of Colonel Pickering's room was ajar. All the drawers and cupboards were open, and his tin trunk was in the middle of the floor. He was packing.

"Hullo," Eliza said in the doorway.

"Thank heavens you're safe."

She came into the room and he kissed her warmly, clutching a pile of shirts. He was the only one who did not ask her, "Where have you been?" He had always treated her as if she had a right to a life of her own.

"Why are you leaving, Colonel Pick?"

"Got to. Higgins has been like a bear with two sore heads, and I — well, it's no fun any more, without you."

"That's kind of you," she said, "to feel like that."

"Frankly, Eliza," he bent with a grunt to

put the shirts in the trunk, "the professor has been just as upset. More so really, because —"

"Missed his dentist," she sniffed. "No one to toast his crumpets."

When she went up to her room, she stood in the doorway for a long time, without moving or changing her expression.

The walls were newly papered with the little delicate rosebuds she and Higgins had seen last time they went shopping. At the window, matching chintz curtains stirred gently in the breeze that filtered through the sweet-smelling lime tree. There was a new rug on the floor, all the paint was freshly white, and the bed was made up with clean sheets and turned down for her to get in.

As if in a dream, Eliza took off her linen dress and left it lying in a crumpled heap on the new rug while she put on her old blue serge skirt with the big buttons and pockets and the white blouse and the blue sailor tie. Moving like a sleepwalker, she went downstairs and into the study. She walked into the exact middle of the carpet to the respiration rose, where she had so often stood and lifted her diaphragm up and down in time to the metronome.

He did not hear her come in. He was standing at the window, looking down at the street. The wax cylinder of the recording machine was turning slowly round under the needle, and out of the speaker came Eliza's voice, slightly out of tune, with all the vowels agonizing.

My old man said, "Foller the van,
And don't dillydally on the wye."
Off went the van wiv me 'ome packed in it . . .

Eliza picked up the song and sang with herself, the two cockney voices blending, so that it was a moment before he turned, a wide smile spreading over his dear face.

. . . You can't trust a special like an old time
    copper
When you can't find your wye 'ome!

"Home," he said. "Home, Eliza."